'*Trenton Makes* boasts the t
a novel of bewitching ingen
melodic mind conceives a w
worthy of that excessive fluo.

New York Times

'A fever dream of a debut novel... By treating gender as
both a choice and a set of social pressures, Koelb offers
a provocative look at how their interaction can shape or
destroy us.'

Times Literary Supplement

'This is a peculiar, gripping book, and Koelb's is a
distinctive voice. Has Kunstler chosen the form his
body must take, or has the society he was born into
chosen it for him? Masculinity and femininity are both
prisons here; and social progress – so-called – comes at
a price. *Trenton Makes* is a fascinating interrogation of
the industrial American dream.'

Financial Times

'The honed-steel sentences on display here – vivid
and sharp and scarily persuasive – are all the more
harrowing for the vulnerability they manage to convey.
Abe Kunstler is a singular protagonist, and *Trenton
Makes* is a passionate and original first novel.'

Garth Risk Hallberg, author of *City on Fire*

TRENTON MAKES

TADZIO KOELB

atlantic·*fiction*

First published in the United States of America in 2018 by Doubleday, a division of Penguin Random House LLC.

First published in Great Britain in hardback in 2018 by Atlantic Books, an imprint of Atlantic Books Ltd.

This paperback edition published in Great Britain in 2019 by Atlantic Books.

1 2 3 4 5 6 7 8 9

A CIP catalogue record for this book is available from the British Library.

Paperback ISBN: 978 1 78649 407 8
EBook ISBN: 978 1 78649 408 5

Printed and bound by CPI Group (UK) Ltd, Croydon, CR0 4YY

Atlantic Books
An Imprint of Atlantic Books Ltd
Ormond House
26–27 Boswell Street
London
WC1N 3JZ

www.atlantic-books.co.uk

Although the characters and events described
in this work are fictional, they are neither without precedent
nor are they so rare as readers might believe.

Man is something that shall be overcome.
What have you done to overcome him?

—FRIEDRICH NIETZSCHE,
THUS SPAKE ZARATHUSTRA

part one

1946–1952

———————————— * ————————————

"The new guy should come, too," Jacks had said in his loud voice, flat as a hand clap, his barrel chest steeped and brimming with all his endless simplicity. Of course the plan had been there all along, but in a way it was Jacks who set the whole thing in motion, because Jacks had said Kunstler should come to the dance hall, and Kunstler had come. It was Jacks, too, who introduced Kunstler to the girl, the taxi dancer, the one called Inez Clay.

"I danced with her," Jacks said, pointing out one girl after another as they swung by with their clients. "And her. And her, I danced with her lots."

"That's a lot of dimes, Jacks. It's like you've danced with every girl in Trenton. No wonder you roll your own." Kunstler's little metallic rasp of a voice was hard to make out over the music, so Jacks had to bend to hear him ask, "What about that one?"

"Oh, that girl? Yeah, I danced with her. The guys say she's got trouble. Kind of like a dipso, they said."

Kunstler lit a cigarette and said, "Like a thing is a thing."

"What?"

"Like a thing is a thing. Someone like a thief is a thief. Someone like a cutup is a cutup. And somebody like a dipso is definitely a dipso. Like just is, there's no difference."

"Yeah, well, she don't go bitching around or anything, I don't think. She just drinks a bit is all." He lowered his voice and said, "Actually the other girls sometimes say that she's kiki, because they figure maybe she don't like men on account of she doesn't like it when the guys get too, well . . . touchy. You know."

"Oh, touchy. Sure, I know," said Kunstler, who instead didn't touch her, or at least not at first, except to shake her hand when Jacks introduced them, calling her "Miss Clay," and later to put a hand on a place high on her back when they danced. Instead he bought her drinks and gave her tickets, which she would rip, turning away to tuck half in the top of her stocking, passing the other half seemingly without looking to a ticket-taker who simply appeared and vanished so quickly again into the crowd that he was little more ever than a reaching hand and a gesture, as if the beaverboard walls with their red-white-and-blue bunting had arms. Then during the band's breaks Kunstler bought her a fresh drink every time and while she drank it they talked—about what, the others couldn't imagine, but she laughed a lot, and when she danced with other clients it seemed that she and Abe Kunstler still found each other's eyes.

The girl was small: that's what caught Kunstler's attention. He wouldn't dance with a tall woman, wouldn't be the little guy with his face buried in some bosom to be laughed at, so the sight of her, petite but not boyish, filling her rayon dress, was a relief. He watched her smile at a factory man still in his cheap war-time woolens and then draw him to the crowded floor, let him stand too close and reach gradually down her back. He also noted the almost invisible retreat by which she baffled his hands when the song was done, no refusal but an evaporation that was also a barrier. She was watery, effortlessly variable, not to be grabbed with fingers. Their first time on the dance floor Kunstler had offered her his right hand and she laughed. He pulled it away.

"Don't be angry," she said.

He nodded. "Mind if we stand—" he started, and she waited and then nodded and whispered, "Away from your friends? Sure." She led him a little way across the hall.

"Now, watch," she demonstrated, moving around him as if he were a spindle, operating his arms. "Open position, here, and now closed position. See? This is how to move for an arm lead. And this is how you move for a body lead."

"Oh, fine," he said. "I won't remember that."

"Don't worry, the names don't mean anything, it's what you do that matters. You'll get it, it's no big deal. This one's not too fast, it will be easy," she said as they started to move away towards the floor. Even then Kunstler was aware how good they looked together, that her softness suited his sharp bones. The girl Inez said, "A few more kisses."

Abe pulled his head back and said, "Sorry, what?"

"The song. 'A Few More Kisses.' I like it. Don't you like it?"

"Sure," he said, "it's swell," but he was concentrating hard on the raised left arm and his right hand at her back, the mirror image, the inverted world, and then they were done, and when her body was gone he was left with a sense he couldn't quite name.

At the end of the night Kunstler waited, ready to help the girl when she stumbled a little drunkenly on the stairs outside the entrance. She asked if he would stop with her in a bar. "The booze at the hall is watered, you know. And I want to listen to some real music. That band's terrible. Everything in that place is terrible. Don't you just love music? I mean real music, good music. Not that stuff they play there." He bought her a gin and Italian, and watched her carry the short brimming glass cautiously to a booth, where she sat without her shoes and sculpting her arches with both hands, saying, "You're never off the clock in those dumps. If you want to even think, you'd better goddamn hop it. They run you sore. You know when we haven't got a fellow we're supposed to dance with each other? Like I'd spend a minute longer with one of those girls than I have to." They sat quietly for a minute, Kunstler neither moving nor speaking, just watching her through the bar darkness with his cast-iron expression. Inez finally said, "Hey, I noticed you work with mostly a lot of Micks. Are you a Catholic?"

"What, me? Oh, hell, I don't know. Maybe. I'm not what I am any more, whatever it is."

"Not a church person, you mean? Me neither." She nodded at that and took a drink before nodding again as if her head rested on the ocean, and said, "I'm Episcopalian. I guess I mean that my mother was."

Then she spoke almost unstoppably, a surge of memories about foster homes where she experienced some things too soon and in overabundance and others not enough. The girl had been fifteen when she accepted her first ticket to dance with a boyish enlisted man at one of the halls near Mountain Home. Both of them had been careful and shy. Back then she drank only Coke and bitters, but of course it was a dance hall, and really they sold two things: the one was illusion, the make-believe of intimacy and gaiety and carelessness. The other was alcohol, which dressed the stage where the illusion could perform. "The pop hurt my stomach after a while," she told him. "Can you believe it, that I had my first cocktail for my health? I always crossed my ankles back then, too. Well, hey, that's life. I mean, what are you going to do?"

It was in Mountain Home that she met the young Bryl-creemed piano player she had followed east. "He was called Boat," the girl said, "on account of he had huge feet, really big. I mean it. He could hardly find anything to fit them. This drummer once said Boat was wrong, he could buy any old shoes and it didn't matter what size, just to wear the box they come in. Isn't that funny?" she asked without laughing. She also described the girl singer they had met at a show in the taxi hall at Millville, a girl whose stockings weren't full of blisters, a girl Boat finally left with, taking with him all the money from the motel room, including all the hard-won nickels that were her fifty percent share of the dimes men paid to dance. "It was mine as much as his, you know. I had to start again, and I'll tell you, it's not easy to save up money at five cents a dance. Someone saw them get in a cab, that's all. That's how I knew they were gone." She looked up at Kunstler, and leaning against him, asked, "Do you think it's because I like spooning more than I like the other stuff? It's not that I don't want to be more like that, more like what it was he hoped for. More what I suppose all men hope for? But things are what they are, I guess. Ever have too much ice cream when you were a kid? A man who was friends with my mother, it was like that with him. The worst part was he made me call him Uncle Andrew."

When at last she relaxed into her gin haze and was quiet Kunstler led her gently to his rooming house, where he checked that the landlord wasn't awake to see him taking her up the stairs.

———————— ⁕ ————————

Jacks had said to them, "The new guy should come, too," and at just that moment everyone, even the ones who might have wanted to argue with him, realized Kunstler was standing right there, the first dressed as usual, silent but at hand, one eye closed against the smoke of his cigarette. *Loitering,* they called it. He stood with his tie knotted tight, one shoulder against his locker door, and nodded his bony face at them as if accepting a compliment, perhaps unaware that they, still open collared or in their undershirts and with their boots next to them on the benches and their socks in their fists, would later agree among themselves that it had been the little man's idea in the first place. "The mouth may be all the way up there where Jacks keeps his head," said Blackie, "but the brain. That's lots closer to the ground, if you know what I mean."

"You're just angry about how he stumps your stupid pranks," Ahern said, and it was true that Kunstler had frustrated them with his imperviousness. Olive pits and sandwich ends and chicken bones and other detritus from their various lunches left in his coverall pockets had been tossed aside so casually you might have thought he generally kept that kind of thing there himself. Blackie and two of the other die men had been especially furious at Kunstler for getting in the way of some practical jokes they played on Jacks, who was mocked for being cheap because he still rolled his own—although of course they knew without having to ask that he didn't make much being only the janitor—and for having not been sent farther than North Carolina during the war, as if he had asked for the posting, or indeed had ever asked in all his life for practically anything.

And yet it wasn't what Kunstler did but the way he had done it that left Blackie so sore. Everything with him went too far, somehow, and without ever being in any way a threat, still it was sinister, like a superstition you know is foolish but frightens you anyway: black cats or thirteen to dinner, an umbrella opened indoors. The first time had been the strangest, when around New Year Blackie, Simmons, and Breen had come back from a weekend skiing, still breathless and hectic, talking and joking, calling to one another over the rhythmic cry of the wire unspooling from coil to capstan to coil. At the lunch hour they had quieted suddenly to watch Jacks walk to the lockers and rummage in his jacket for cigarette papers. He thought to look before he started rolling only because of how they stood—clustered, alert—and having tumbled to them he held his paper up to the blunt electric light and saw someone had drawn a long and knotted penis, which he would then have put in his mouth.

"How do you like it?" one of them asked him. "Balls first or tip first?"

"Remember you have to lick it to make it sticky," said Blackie.

Jacks crumpled the thin strip into his coverall pocket straight away, nodding around with a half smile and saying, "Okay, okay," in his flush monotone. He pulled out another paper—only that, too, was part of the gag, because he had almost shaken out his tobacco before he noticed it was the same. In fact, as he peeled away one after another he found all the papers were ruined: they had drawn the same thing on every one and placed them carefully back in the box. Blackie and the others laughed out loud now. "That took us all weekend," Breen said. "You should appreciate the hard work." The emphasized word *hard* made them laugh again.

"How am I going to smoke?"

"You're just going to have to chew that over."

"Har, har. Come on, give me a cig."

"Sorry, Jackson. I think we're all out."

It was then that Kunstler had appeared suddenly from his leaning place against the wall, and taking the little cardboard envelope from Jacks stood for a moment looking at it, flipping through the papers with all the lack of interest or hurry of someone looking through a book in a foreign language. "That's funny," the little man said in his high, croaking metal wheeze, a voice that always sounded as if it were being cranked out on a rusty machine. Then, still holding the papers, he said with the same absolutely humorless manner, the same patina of calm, "Hey, here's a funny one for you. These three guys, they go skiing, but they're just factory slobs, like us, no money. So they share a room, the three of them. Then there's just the one bed, but that's no problem, they can share that, too. Fine. And in the morning, the one on the left says, 'It's crazy, I dreamed some guy was whacking me off,' and the guy on the right says, 'Hey, I had the same dream.'" While Kunstler spoke he let the papers drop snow-like to the floor and offered Jacks a pre-rolled from his coverall pocket. He went on, Jacks leaning down expectantly, the others already gathering their anger. "So the guy in the middle, he says, 'You two are nuts. I just dreamed I was skiing.'" Unsmiling, he lit a match against the wall, barely raising it to Jacks' dipped cigarette.

"Jesus, that crazy bastard," Blackie had said when it became clear Kunstler was going to let the thing burn right down to his fingernail. Jacks had been laughing too hard; he hadn't noticed.

"Hey, tell us another one," said Jacks, his cigarette still unlit in his hand.

"Maybe later," Kunstler said. He dropped the burnt-out match and walked away.

When the whistle had gone, Kunstler, his thumbnail blistered a screaming painful black from the match, stood by the exit with his hands lost in his pockets, and didn't move or even look around as the others passed him; he was waiting for Jacks the way a man waits for a bus, and waiting for Jacks to say, "Hey, do you want to go for a drink?" so that Kunstler, lighting a cigarette and handing one to Jacks, reaffirming their private currency, could say, "I guess so," and follow to a bar. They went to a place not too far from the factory, a narrow alley of dark wood and tin panels that had been painted until their patterns were almost lost. The place had no stools. Men stood here and drank, and if they were too tired to stand, they went home. It was busy after the shift, and at the counter they waited a while for the bartender. Jacks strained his neck the whole time looking for whoever else they might know.

"'I dreamed I was skiing,'" said Jacks. "That's a good one.

It took me a minute. I guess maybe you know a lot of them like that."

"I guess. All of them, some of them. I don't know. A few."

"I guess Blackie seemed pretty sore that you got the big laugh, when he thought it was him would be needling me."

"Well, he was falling anyway. I just pushed because I could."

"How do you mean?"

"Nothing, forget it."

"Hey, order me a whiskey," Jacks told Kunstler, and walked a few steps away to look around.

When the barman came Kunstler held up two fingers and said, "Whiskey."

"Water, soda?" said the barman. Kunstler felt blank, but steadily looked at him across the counter. He took his hand out of his pocket and put it carefully on the bar's scuffed wooden edge, dollar ready between forefinger and thumb, but the barman simply repeated himself, only louder, the words knuckled, "Mister, straight, water, or soda?" and waited. "Right," Kunstler said without expression, but found the barman still didn't move, and so added, "Soda." The barman went away. When the drinks arrived Jacks returned to the bar, where he paid by tossing his dollar bill at the counter, and then Kunstler tossed his, too, so that it landed almost on the first and was immediately caught and taken by the barman and replaced with coins. Holding their glasses Kunstler and Jacks stood with their backs against the zinc-topped bar and looked at the grey winter light coming through the half-glass door. The big man's flushed face shook and nodded to the sound of the radio but Kunstler barely moved his head at all; only his eyes turned as the other drank, their movement hard and hidden, and when Jacks had taken a sip and not complained or made a face but simply kept up a gentle springing to the rhythm, Kunstler drank, and to himself repeated: *Soda. Whiskey and soda. Soda.* He bought the next two rounds. Jacks said, "Hey, you buying me all these drinks. Thanks," and Kunstler answered, "Hell, it never hurts to be friends with the big guy."

"I'm sure big," Jacks said in his unmodulated yell, standing up and puffing out his chest. Kunstler laughed—a light tipsy fluting—but stopped right away.

It wasn't the first time Kunstler had drunk too much, but it had been a long while—too long, he decided, since like everything it was a skill—and then it had been different before, when it wasn't him yet, and someone else had been there to steer the blinded ship, then later share the pain. When he woke up the blurred clock read nearly five-fifteen. The way he felt, he wasn't sure he'd wound it. The only way he even knew for sure he had gone to bed was because that's where he woke up. He experienced a moment of terrible panic: he tried to remember what he had done. Had he said something he shouldn't? He still had his shirt on. That reassured him, somehow. His thumb ached with burning.

In the bathroom on the landing the key was turned as carefully as ever in the lock, but otherwise it was all a rush: he dumped his razor and mug and brush in the yellowed bowl, and while he dressed he ran the tap so they all got good and wet. He lathered just enough cream out of the mug to tuck some with his fingertip behind his left ear. As he was about to turn the key again to leave he realized he had made a mistake. With his hands he wet the towel, too—in the middle, and taking care not to over-do it. Consistency and details: these were the things that kept him safe. A clean-shaven man must have his elements—a foamy brush, a wet razor; on the peg he leaves a humid towel just as surely as a passing car leaves tracks in snow. Kunstler let the door slam behind him as he went down the stairs two at a time.

In his street he just walked—quickly but not too quickly, because to rush, he knew, was to invite attention, recollection, investigation—until he turned a corner and the boardinghouse was out of sight; then he ran through the hunched, aluminum-sided streets. He ran all the way to the grassy strip that edged the train tracks, and after looking to see that no one was there to observe him in the growing light, ran on and over the short hill. Stumbling up the embankment muddied his knees, and for a moment it felt as if the edge of the fence where he ducked under might have ripped his jacket. He didn't wait, though, as this was the only chance he had before work started, and in a moment it would arrive, and a moment later be gone, even if it felt like forever while the noise of it was in his chest, and he knew that consistency was everything, had learned once from a door heart-stoppingly ajar to a diner men's room that nothing could be forgotten, not for a day or an hour, not even for just a minute, because the world was an eye that never blinked. He must be the same in all things: unvaried in his voice, just as in his walk or his clothes. *Nothing can change.* The sound was coming already as he slid down to the tracks where the grass seemingly trembled in anticipation of the approaching wind. He bent with his hands on his knees to catch the breath he had spent on running. Then with all of a machine's thundering furious uniformity of sound and motion the Pennsy rushed past, drowning everything, and while it was there, the shattering storm of it all around him, he screamed as loud as he could, arms seized to his sides by effort, lost in the godly mechanical noise until the muscles of his face and throat and chest burned and recoiled and refused to scream any more. Then the train was gone and the wind and passion with it; there was emptiness and silence in its place. He found his hat ten yards away. Later he threw up his first cup of coffee and it smelled like booze.

He had worked other jobs at first—menial, small, unskilled, and uninteresting. He had been testing, trying, but especially learning from the men, the Greek waiters and the colored busboys, the customers who ate every day sitting on vinyl stools at plastic counters without speaking or removing their hats, who told dirty jokes and drank their coffee while they chewed, who threw their ties over their shoulders when they had soup and carried the paper in their suit pockets. Their badges were crusts of dried shaving soap and hair oil and bluntness and the endless scratching between their legs. He watched them, cautiously but closely, especially the occasional ones who showed up still in uniform, making their way back from France or the Philippines or wherever the war had taken them, eating and drinking and dancing up their last few weeks of service pay ten cents at a time with the irrepressible cheer of men taken off guard at coming home alive.

Despite the fears that shook him, no one back then had ever asked him for anything except his name. Saying it the first time out loud drove an edgeless hole of panic through his chest. He had been repeating it to himself every waking hour for days, said nothing else to anyone, a prayer to a lost god that he had begun reciting the minute he saw the hand-written advertisement in the diner window, *help Wanted,* and repeated endlessly, chant-like, in a frenzy of postponement. It was hunger that had driven him back to the diner as if at the point of a knife. He was almost disappointed to find the card still in the window: it meant he had been cursed with luck and would have to go ahead with his plan, see it through. He would not that easily escape the accident that defined him.

Eventually he added to the name, expanded on the abbre-viated chronicle that was contained in the words *Abe Kunstler.* He gave only the barest bones, but they were enough over time to sketch the man's story. He told one boss that he had been in the service, and seen action. He told another that he had been a POW. One day with the anticipation of an inven-tor at last switching on a long-planned machine, he gave it the final embellishment, the portion that was his, that made him who he was, the truth setting him apart from what was otherwise just a name and the rest: the injury, the physical evidence of his person, testimony to his past and patent on his future—that he had been wounded in the war. He would say it just that way: *wounded. I was wounded in the war.*

In between there had been the man in the dirty white side cap and apron who said, "Kraut name, right? My grand-mother's family was Kraut. I don't speak it or nothing," and let him work in the back in a cloud of steam and all-enveloping grease. There Kunstler washed the thick dishes in great galvanized tubs, handing them in stacks for drying to a colored boy a decade or more older than he was. The aproned man with the Kraut grandmother let him eat there, too, the special and a coffee, one meal a day. It wasn't the factory, but it was a good enough place to start, so he worked hard, never asking for a day off or an advance on the week. He stayed until the afternoon someone told a dirty joke, and with the other men he had laughed. The light, tittering sound was a frightening call from the past. Hearing it, he did the only thing he could think of, which was just what he would have done if he had seen or imagined seeing struck in someone's face even the smallest spark of recognition, anything that risked burning down the still rough-timbered façade he was constructing: he walked straight for the door, letting fall his apron as he went, saying not a word to anyone, looking at nobody, and never going back.

Other, similar jobs followed, given to him by similar men in similarly soiled counter clothes, with similar voices and faces and lives, who offered him the same stiff, flat kindness, impersonal and uninflected. They employed similar short-order cooks who asked Kunstler in the same teasing tones why he didn't have a girl. One even paid for the driver's test so he could make deliveries. Each time he remained, with no plan to leave, until some panic took him, whether a fear of his own creeping sense of ease or comfort, or something more immediate like the laughing he should never have done. Then he would walk out, saying nothing, leaving his last pay uncollected, just as he had the first time, forgetting the places almost as soon as he left them, thinking only of the next.

There had been, too, the local teens who mocked his high voice and called him a flower, who once threw stones as he walked away from them down the road until he turned at last and for no reason he could ever name or understand but still knew somehow to be right took a fistful of dirt from the soft shoulder and threw it in his own face, and then another, screaming all the while, a long wordless choking scream, until the boys, scared and shocked, called him crazy and ran away, leaving him frightened and hoarse, but knowing now the sound of his new voice.

He was always aware that he could never fight them, of course, not these boys or any others like them, whatever the provocation: for him there could be no police, no frisk, no night in the tank, no common toilet or shower, just as there could be no swimming pools, no hospitals, no examinations or confidences or unguarded laughter—a list too long of things kept in a room whose door hung ready at any moment to swing open in a disaster of exposure.

·

Ten and a half miles away they were laying rope and drawing wire. It was too far for any of the factory men to eat where he worked, but sometimes when he got an afternoon off Kunstler took the bus out, then walked the unpeopled warehouse road and stood by the gate to watch them. It wasn't like the factory he knew. The floor wasn't as big, and it looked to him as if maybe they weren't making anything bigger than elevator cable, nothing that could hold a bridge certainly, but anyway that was fine: drawing wire was drawing wire. He told himself that soon enough he would be on the floor again. He would go to them when he was ready, and in his body he sensed now that he was very nearly ready, that the next time he walked out on a job, this is where he would go. He would be ready or he wouldn't: he couldn't wait forever.

But first there had been the day when one of the waitresses had asked him if he wouldn't like to take her out, maybe next weekend, maybe to see a picture, and for that reason there was the heavily spectacled salesclerk in dandruffed vest and shirtsleeves who said as Kunstler, his savings in his pocket, stood hesitantly in the doorway of a flyblown shop: "Specials today. Part-worsted gabardine pinstripe suit thirteen ninety-five." He told him how many pieces were in the sharkskin suit, because it came with extra trousers and was available in medium blue or medium brown, special at eleven ninety-five in English Terylene that wouldn't fade or wrinkle, and about the casual corduroy sport coat and part-worsted gabardine hound's-tooth slacks eleven fifty for the set. He kept going until Kunstler was lost in the words, unable to set them to images, as if they were just musical notes. "Now's the time to shop," the clerk said, "have the place to yourself," and when Kunstler wavered, he added, "We don't get a lot of business during the week, frankly. Buy a suit today and, well . . . what? I'll throw in a tie." The clerk's thick glasses were split across the middle and his eyes, partitioned, looked like dark yolks loosed from black eggs, or fish slipping through a bowl. The lenses tossed the sun in Kunstler's face so that he was briefly blind as he entered the woody dimness of the store. When the space at last ripened out of the feathered dark he was standing in the middle of a small carpet facing a mirror.

"Arms at your sides, please," the clerk said. "Relaxed." He pulled a tape measure from over his neck and passed it down Kunstler's arm, and then pressed it across his back. Kunstler got tense. "First time fitted?" the clerk asked.

"I guess so."

"It won't hurt at all, I promise," the man said. "I must have measured half the men in this town, I guess. Or at least half the ones now over thirty, to be specific. Times are changing; everything is changing. Department stores, you know. There's Bamberger's everywhere now, Epstein's, too. Hard to compete. Their service isn't like what you get here, of course, but it seems no one has time these days. Arms up, please."

Kunstler lifted his arms and then started as the tape measure passed around his chest, but the clerk did no more than incline his head in a brief bow, and then proceed about his work, Kunstler aware but somehow not nervous, watching the man run his thick glasses close over the black and yellow measurements and then against the slip of paper where he wrote them down with a stub of pencil.

After measuring Kunstler's neck the man stopped and pursed his lips. "Well, fourteen," the clerk said, lifting his tortoiseshells and double-checking his thumbnail against the tape measure with a closely pressed bare eye. "Fourteen, fourteen. We don't stock fourteens much, frankly," he remarked. "No one around here does, I don't think. That is unless, unless. Unless . . ." He took the word away with him into the rear of the shop, leaving behind a pleasant, church-like quiet. Kunstler slowly put his arms down. He enjoyed this, he realized, enjoyed looking at the racks and the shelves, feeling a part of this place, this thing. Then the clerk reappeared with a small stack of folded shirts, mostly pale blue and yellow.

"We used to carry some boys' . . . well. Younger men's clothes. Sometimes people wanted something more formal for confirmations, weddings, that kind of thing, you know. Here's what we have left. The styles are a little dated, frankly, as we don't have much call any more, but I think we'll find something to fit you, and I can give you a good price on it. It's really just taking up shelf room, you see? The owner'll be just as glad to have the space as the merchandise." He piled them on the counter. "I brought some ties from back there, too. I worry these others would trail you like a noose." He put a set of ties in Kunstler's hand and asked, "Left or right?"

Kunstler looked briefly into the bottle-bottom specs with behind them the wheeling, impassive eye-fish and then at the lines and loops of the ties before saying, with something less than conviction, "Right." The clerk with some effort got down on one knee. Kunstler jumped when the clerk pressed the tape to the inside of his left leg, but again the clerk ignored him, keeping up a hum of small talk about recent styles and changing clientele as he measured and then climbed his way upright, and while he talked Kunstler looked down at the oiled grey hair with its salting of white flakes as if seeing a mountain range from the cloud tops. The clerk said, "For the suit I think we can get away with a thirty-four. I don't have a lot of them, to tell you the truth, but more choice than you'll have for the shirts. Or you can go to a department store, maybe Atlantic Mills, but you'll be limited to what's in the boys', I should think, if you'll forgive me for saying so. Anyway, it's up to you. You want I should pull out the thirty-fours?"

Then after, in the pure, smooth mirror, with the cream shirt and the grey suit, the printed tie, the long tabs of collars, Kunstler found a presence unmistakable, stronger even than the evidence of a disloyal body—not mere mask, it seemed to him then, but substance. Gone would be the confining sense of materials inappropriate, cladding that would not embrace the structure, the cursed lack of rightness in the matter by which he was bound. Instead he saw a real man, with all of a man's despicable, admirable arrogance and strength of body—an image that would not remain merely an image.

The clerk was still talking, saying, "That fits pretty well, I'd say, wouldn't you? Cuff the leg, of course, shorten the sleeves a little bit, and it's just right, really. Want me to make the alterations?"

"I guess I'll do it . . . I mean, I'll ask my land-lady to take care of it for me."

"There's no charge for alterations, you know."

"No, but I guess she'll be happy to do it and then I won't have to find the time to come back."

"As you like. Have far to go? I'll box it. Oh, don't worry about folds, you'll see—that suit will barely wrinkle at all. Just hang it for a day. Everything will drape right out."

Kunstler decided at the last minute to trade his soft cap for a felt Dunlap that wasn't really the right color but happened to fit. "Trust me," said the clerk. "Whatever the ads say, even a good hat will change plenty once the weather gets right in it a couple of times, and this one, well: maybe a little faster than that, even." He handed over a deep cardboard box filled with tissue paper and cloth, tied with white and red twine.

Kunstler wore the hat, one fearful hand on the brim in case there should be any wind, and carried his cap in his jacket pocket. There was enough money left over to practice buying tickets to the picture show. None of the titles meant anything to him, so he took a seat for whatever was playing next. The first was a western, the second a musical, with between them the newsreels and cartoons; each seemed as remote and brittle as the other, a series of indistinguishable poses struck behind a silvered window, colored vapors noised by distant, undersea voices, echoes upon echoes. For nearly four hours he sat and stared at the nothingness, then went home to the lodging house, where he basted the suit's cuffs and looked with wonder at its beauty, and thought how it would roll over him as close and as enduring as a shadow.

There was no hot water at the lodging house so before his date he knocked off work a little early and washed up in the restroom at the diner. Stripped to his shorts, barefoot and air cool in the tiled room, he observed in the mirror the prominent ribs, the waxy yellowed knobs of shoulder and elbow, studied almost with the distant curiosity of a passing stranger the press and gear of muscle and bone and tendon as he scrubbed at his neck and underarms with fingernails foamed on the cracked cake of pink soap.

His bandages were only half on again when he noticed in the reflected room behind his own inverted face the open door—open just a little, hardly anything: but he knew that even a little was too much. There was no one there that he could see, but the door was open when it hadn't been, shouldn't have been; by that crack it swung open on his every fear, and in the grip of that fear he slammed it violently shut. Over the sounds of the kitchen being cleaned for the night it was impossible to hear if someone was there waiting, or walking away, but the door had not been closed. Had he never closed it? Could it have opened by itself? He felt sure it had been shut. Had it not been shut? *I have not been careful,* he thought. *I have not taken care.* It was not hard for him to imagine an eye, a shocked face. *Someone has seen me,* he thought next, *and everything is already done and lost.* He began to sweat. There was an image in his mind of police, of the lights flashing from their cars, and for a moment he wished his were a different name. While he finished his bandages, pulling tighter than ever as if there were protection to be found in them, he held the closed door in place by sitting on the toilet and pushing with one foot. Then he put on his new clothes, the suit that not so long ago had seemed a monument to his triumph and was now perhaps the cause of his absolute destruction. He pressed his back against the door while he kneeled to pack his old clothes in the suit's box. He was aware of his heart's rhythm.

After a deep breath he turned to the closed door that led from the restroom back to the place where the others—the cook and the counter girl, the busboy, the owner, the customers who sat on the vinyl stools or in the booths and waited now for something, food or revelation—either knew or didn't. He was safe or exposed, alive or dead. He stood with one hand on the door handle and the other holding tight to the package, stayed that way for a moment, thinking about what would come next, what might be on the other side, an image of police arriving, of a desperate attempt at escape. When his breath returned, he clenched his jaw tight and turned the knob.

Finding no one waiting for him in the hall, he made a decision. He would not walk towards the front, where expecting him there was either a waitress ready for an evening at the pictures or else a room full of anger and disgust and recrimination, bunched fists and possibly worse. Instead he made his way straight out the back, into the alley behind, where the garbage was kept. He deposited the suit box in the trash there. Then he walked, steadily but not fast, to the lodging house. He didn't look back or around or even really in front of him: he moved in a kind of daze that mingled gradually with the evening's dark. He had no bag so he put his shaving things and underclothes into one of the land-lady's pillowcases. He tied it tight, tucked it under his arm, and left.

He lay that night on a bench in the bus station, expecting that someone would appear with the annunciation of his fraudulence as spotted through the open bathroom door, tried to accept that he would soon be seized and destroyed; but it didn't happen. No one came in but some salesmen with their sample cases and a janitor who cleaned around him as if he weren't there. In the morning he took the bus out to the factory and with the same chanting focus as before he practiced again, this time the whole story, the encapsulation of who he was and always now would be: "My name is Abe Kunstler. I was a soldier and a POW. I can draw wire, and I was wounded in the war."

When they gave him the job he told himself, *Somehow despite all my mistakes I have made it here, and now at last I am home.* He felt certain then that his plan must be a kind of destiny.

———————————— • ————————————

"That bastard is crazy," Blackie complained to Ahern.

"Let me tell you something. You played a prank, which apparently he didn't care for. He told a joke, which apparently you didn't care for, any more than he did. As far as I can see, there isn't anything else to it than that."

"Come on. You don't like that little jerk any more than I do."

"You're probably right," said Ahern. "I don't. But the way I figure, I would rather know why, and it don't have a god-damn thing to do with his dirty jokes or your box of dirtied cig papers."

It was after the incident with the papers that someone decided to go squealing to the floor manager, which was considered unthinkable, a break in the ranks they held as sacred as they might any sworn bond. The snitch claimed that Kunstler always seemed to be dressed by the time the others had barely opened their lockers. "We're just punching out, and he shows up with his pansy tie all tied and his hat already on his head and a smoke in his puss. Some of the guys think he changes in the john."

"So maybe he's shy, so what?" the floor manager asked.

"So then he stands there and just watches us."

"Watching you is hardly a crime, I hope," the floor manager said. "Myself, I only do it for the money. I hope you'll understand, not take it the wrong way."

"Who's joking? You know what I mean. He's slipping out. He leaves the floor early, while the rest of us are still at it."

"While the rest of you are still yakking, you mean. Kunstler's not the one wasting time around here. He's the first one on the floor in the morning, I might point out. Clocks in and out right, every time, I might point out. Never late back from breaks."

"You might point out."

"Hey, you're catching on fine. You think maybe I don't check the cards? Brother, you're wrong. You get here twenty minutes early every day, you can be ready to punch the minute the whistle goes, too. You can even change in the john, if you like." They figured the manager liked Kunstler because he didn't need much training: the little man had walked in off the street dressed as he always was when not in his coverall, his clothes not expensive but too new, his tie too loud and his collar points too long, with a cigarette in his mouth the whole time and one eye closed against the smoke, and announced in his voice like scraping rust that he could draw wire.

"You look a little young," the manager said, to which Kunstler only shrugged.

"Maybe," he said. "But I can still draw wire."

The manager walked the little man to a machine and around it. Butler was working it but the manager nodded at him and so he handed his gloves to the manager, who handed them to Kunstler. Kunstler accepted them inattentively and set about topping the powder in the stuffing boxes. Then he lit a new cigarette out of his pocket and waited silently for the spool to empty. When the new spool arrived, he turned to the manager and said, "Conditioned?" and the manager nodded, but Kunstler checked the wire anyway with his thumb before he strung it up, easing the work through the first lube box and die and then around the capstan, through the second block, and on around the machine. He handed the manager back the gloves and then stood by the receiving coil for a minute to watch for seams, his hands in his suit coat pockets, his cigarette in the corner of his mouth.

"You lay rope?" the manager asked. Kunstler dropped his butt on the floor and stepped on it before he shook his head and said, "Not me. I just draw wire."

"Rod? Bar?"

"I guess maybe I could, but not really. Wire's what I know."

"Where do you work now?"

"Nowhere. I was in the service. I might have lied to them about my age. I've been out a bit now."

"And since?"

They watched the wire run through the blocks to the spool for a moment and then Kunstler shrugged again. "Lot of nothing," he said. "More or less." Then he talked about being in the POW camp, and how there was an accident, and how he had been hurt. *Wounded* was the word he used. The manager nodded.

"Okay," the manager said.

The next day Kunstler was there before anyone else, ready to work, and work was all he did, hardly talking, barely even looking at the others, just waving wordlessly to the man who worked the trolley when it was time to spider the finished wire onto the drum. They didn't have a coverall small enough for him at first, so he wore an old one with the sleeves and legs cut down, and the name O'Brien on the patch. He taped the wrists and ankles shut so they wouldn't get caught in the works.

"They like him upstairs because he's just one more machine," Foley said. "That's why they let him get dolled up to come in and stare at the rest of us dressing."

"Le dernier cri," said Augie, who had been stationed in Paris.

Blackie said, "That and his spiel about being a POW. I bet you he carries his draft card in his pocket, along with his dog tags and the box number for his CO."

"Probably sleeps with his service pin under his pillow."

"Did you ever hear him talk about it? Says, 'I was wounded in the war.' Everyone else gets shot, or stabbed, or blown up. Something normal that they can goddamn name. But Abe Kunstler? No, not him. He gets himself *wounded.*" Blackie was getting steamed, too steamed, or at least so it seemed to Butler, who stood up at that, and asked, "Any of you get captured and taken to Germany? He was in a camp, he got cut up like a piece of fruit from what I understand he told the foreman, so for all I care the guy can call it wounded and a boo-boo and whatever the hell else he wants."

Everyone was quiet, because they all knew that in 1944 Butler had spent seven days locked in a shit-filled cattle car from Belgium to Poland with fifty other men. Not all of them survived the trip but it hadn't always been possible to tell because they were packed in so tight that the dead didn't necessarily fall, but swayed on with the others as if feigning life. Everyone had heard, although always with the courtesy not to remember where, that he still woke up with nightmares. Then Bobby, the young guy who worked the winder, said that he had come in early once and found Kunstler putting on his gear, and seen clearly visible beneath his undershirt the blue-edged beige bandage around his ribs. Kunstler hadn't said anything as he finished buttoning himself into his coverall, not a word, just watched Bobby, who in shame or fear or something else it would have been hard for him to name had looked away. "I almost felt like he was daring me to say something to him about it," Bobby said. And Butler, still standing, looking down at a grease rag he was worrying now in his hand, said, "He could walk around here with that scar showing all the time, give you something really shocking to start at. Instead he just dresses solitary, like, on his own. You should all lay off him for a while, give him a break. Give us all a goddamn break."

That put an end to it, although in a sense it had been ended long before, because as Blackie said, "That was some day, when Kunstler pulled the thorn out of Jackson's paw." Jacks was already and forever the means through which Kunstler communicated with the rest of the floor, the wedge by which he pried open the unyielding shell of their society, because although the others might have treated Jacks to pranks and thought of him as a kind of servant and even called him *poor dumb Jacks* without always checking first to be sure he wasn't there to hear, they felt for him that automatic sense of ownership that sometimes comes from knowing someone too long to consider it any sort of choice. Soon enough they felt something similar for Kunstler, too, came to think of him as theirs alone to disparage, although it's likely that not one of them at any point realized it, and certain that not one of them would have admitted it in any case if he had. That was why nearly a year after he had first showed up they still called him the new guy, no matter how many others had come since, and it was also why, when Jacks said, "The new guy should come, too," no matter what anyone else thought they wanted, no one argued about it, and in the end he came, the new guy, Abe Kunstler, accompanying them to the dance hall.

.

Unclothed and boozy on Kunstler's narrow bed beneath the unshielded bulb the girl was a bright, creamy pool, braced by the cool air, and he skimmed the goosed surface with his small, factory-stained hand while they kissed, watched the tips of her breasts pucker and rise. Released from the amending circumstance of her clothing she was more than ever a girl, the unwrinkled youthfulness of her body, stubby and blunt as a kitten's, almost shocking. She stroked his face and they stayed like that for a while, Kunstler sitting on the edge of the bed, the girl Inez setting slowly into half sleep and the mess of unwashed bedclothes beneath his moving hand. "Spooning is what I like the best," she admitted again, "but I like the rest well enough when I've had something to drink." He had given her plenty to drink, but still he was not aggressive. He looked her in the eye and made each movement of his hand slow, taking a long while before finally with a spit-wet finger he unpicked the gate of hair woven between her legs.

This was the distorted mirror of his imagination come to life, a moment he had pictured and which had looked so much like this in thought, but which now in acting had expanded dangerously beyond control: for of course he had not dreamed far enough, and when she reached awkwardly to open his shirt, Kunstler pulled away so suddenly in his surprise that he slipped to the floor and hit his back on the wall with a force that nearly winded him. Panic and confusion cast the girl out of her twilight, and she seemed abruptly aware of her nakedness, bunched what could be reached of the sheet between her legs with one arm, and wrapped the other around her breasts.

It took her a moment of looking around as if to get her bearings to ask, "What's wrong? What's the matter?" He didn't respond and she asked again, then again, her voice starting to rise: "What's wrong? What is it?"

Kunstler said, "Wait, just wait."

"I don't understand what's going on," she said. "I don't understand."

He struck the floor with his palm and said, "Wait, now," and she started, and he said, "Look, okay?" Then he said, "Look, but wait."

Slowly then he lifted his undershirt to display a broad section of tightly wrapped medical bandage, the blue edges crisscrossed, bright safety pin beneath his arm, telling her at first only what he had told the factory others when Jacks kidded him for always being first into the locker room, an explanation that had been brief, reticent, almost angry, a wire-like barrier of hostile sensitivity, hardly more than an admission that something was different, that he had been hurt—although *wounded* was the word he had used in speaking to the foreman: *I was wounded in the war.* "Not fighting," he said. "Prisoner-of-war camp, inside Germany." His look and his tone had challenged everyone to take this as explanation enough. He anyway had nothing more to tell them. There was no story: there was just the wound.

Now, however, sitting on the floor across from the naked girl wrapped for safety in her own arm, Kunstler suddenly knew the history of his misfortune in a strange and easy detail that before had eluded him, and he spoke to himself however much it sounded as if he were speaking to her, because to speak was to explore it, stake it out, talking with growing urgency and almost satisfaction of it all, of the camp where the soldiers had been taken and of their misery, of his injury, his consciousness held suddenly captive by the words he found. Confused and indistinct events in being told became clear, durable, and he experienced anew the original era of his being, the strange countryside like the landscape in a dream, the body found dismembered by a bomb in a clearing between the birch trees, followed now by panic and failed flight from capture. Then the details, apprehended as if through a keyhole, commandeered: that there had been Negro men at the camp, dozens of them, more than the man had ever seen in one place before, and darker than he had ever seen, too, their vein-streaked eyes a permanent shock in the night of their faces, who spoke French and had French names, and who were luckier in that at least than the man had been with his German name for which the others distrusted him. There were Russians, too, beyond a double line of fence, treated worse than all the rest, who got hardly anything more than a half bucket of potatoes to eat between them and lived on the cold floors of their tents, anticipatory retribution meted out for the horrible but expected revenge they would and did exact when the Reds marched in and it was the turn of the camp guards to attempt a terrified escape. Kunstler heard again but in his own voice for the first time the forgotten names the man had brought back from Germany: *Stalag III-A and Luckenwalde. Brandenburg. Markendorf.*

The men held in these names were no longer soldiers. "They weren't even really men, any more," Kunstler told her. They were just struggling and wasting bodies, the person inside driven out, missing, refuged elsewhere and perhaps never coming back. To the Germans they were less maybe even than that: they were enemies and prisoners, which is to say, little more than tools if they were anything at all other than a burden, and so to justify their right to a physical form they were made to work. There were factories outside the camp, each with machines to run, fires to stoke, crates to lift and stack, then lift again. Guards drove the prisoners from the camp in frozen canvas-covered trucks to buildings all across Brandenburg.

Kunstler knew it had been a fertile place, trees thick along the edges of villages and fields, solid and venerable, a landscape strong with the strength of things that live through winter—but he could not see any of that now. In his mind instead he and the dozen faceless others and their silhouetted guards traveled on the half-open flatbed across a brown-grey and dusty plain, a place ever-withered and leafless, deciduous, hard, where wind blew down endless miles of road and railway, and he imagined that from the truck they had watched trains roll by filled with the things they had made with their soulless hands in the factories for their captors, otherwise safe, otherwise normal things—buttons, metal knobs, lightbulbs, things that might be and likely were here, right now, in the building where they lay, the girl on the bed, half naked in her sheet and loosening arm, he on the floor with his bandages exposed. They were everywhere, in fact: in every building he could think of, the factories and the stores and the bars, and though he knew they were harmless, the sight of them in his dream of dust and tarmac brought on such a feeling of disgust that they might have been the organs and limbs of the dead.

The factory, too, he saw differently than he knew it must have been: not the high, lofted hangars as housed the great spools of wire rope, but rather a low, long building of orange brick with a tiled roof, and rising from the center a square turret under which the train line ran. It was as still in his mind as a photo, so that however long his thoughts approached along the beckoning tracks, it grew no closer.

The prisoners, weak and cold and set to using unfamiliar machines under managers they couldn't understand, were often hurt and sometimes even killed in the unwilling, lethargic rush to make and build, but kept here in the middle of Germany, what else were they going to do? There was no running, no escape, and if ever someone tried to get away, retribution fell on all of them who remained. Those who couldn't work might be beaten as punishment for their hunger and exhaustion, and so they drove their empty, manless bodies from which the souls had flown frightened like ducks from a gunshot and tried hard as they worked not to think of the crates filling with the phantom limbs that were lightbulbs or buttons or rivets or springs. To make these things they lost fingers and eyes, burned their skin, crushed the bones in their feet.

Kunstler's accident involved a furnace, he told the girl quietly, its rage only barely contained by the hatch, a pyre-in-waiting wrapped in a hazy shroud of coal-dust and heat, and now from sternum to thigh he was misshapen, reduced and distorted by the needs of the machine. Speaking of his body and the furnace, he thought of blood, the compliant procession of liquid from wound, *the slow dark lake,* how long it took to dry. He heard the deathly knock of bone, and to drive the sound of it from his mind he described the room again: the trapdoor cut by a daylight strip that led to the road but not freedom, the burning world behind the boiler door, and himself condensed until he was nothing more than his circumstances: a thing spectral, empty.

Through the memory he heard her, Inez, the naked milky girl, the puddle of pale skin and alcohol: she was crying for him, which he had never done for himself, and saying things—trite, calming things, the kind he would never allow himself to think or say, the kind he hated but knew must have their place somewhere: "It's a part of you," she said. "It's part of what makes you who you are."

From just where he found himself on the floor, his back still against the wall, he accepted to hold her outstretched hand. When her breathing calmed at last he rose and carefully laid the blanket over her and spread his coat on top of that, and watched as in the morning light she slept.

Kunstler moved quietly from beside the heavy-breathing body and switched off the lamp that sat on the floor beside the bed. Once inside the bathroom on the landing he carefully turned the key in the lock, then twisted the handle of the door once to be sure. *Part of you,* the girl Inez called his disfigurement in her weeping, but she had been upset to see the bandages that bound his chest, and for a time he let the words infuriate him: he would never accept pity, he told himself, not from anyone—and yet, when in the locked bathroom Kunstler took off his shirt and unwrapped the bandages, slipped off his trousers and drawers and then the athletic supporter, when he stood fully naked and looked gravely down at himself—he now, and no longer the she that once was, but still possessing the subjugated and forgotten breasts, and between his legs the tufted furrow with its despised bleeding that must be hidden—he felt a pain and thought, *This has been no lie: it was me, really me, who was wounded in the war.* On his fingers was the smell of the girl, intimate and distant, known but alien, the strange line between self and another and also between past and present, the odor of the wound he suffered, of the most private part of him, the most personal, unshared and unsharable, to be kept among those beating, pumping places within the body that you can't expose and survive. *Yes,* he thought: *I was wounded in the war.*

Naked in the locked bathroom, dizzied by the smell of the girl and the incandescent desire it had imported furtively from the bed, he sat on the rolled lip of the tub. The perfumed hand covered his face; the other he put to his body, a pilgrimage to his earlier self that he resented but that was also essential, natural somehow to the man he had become.

Not yet he but the she that once was thought, I never sought it out. *The transference of power, of kind, to overthrow him, even in his failure, had not been her place until the man her husband presented it to her, carved it from that which had been his own, and she accepted, found it not just open but demanding, an emptiness wishing and whimpering to be filled. So when he raised his hand she saw that he was pointing also to the coming end, that the blow she would once have considered it her natural duty to accept was now an invitation, and she knew that it would be a mercy to release him, so that when his weakness itself called to her with a fishy slap across the face she was ready to answer it with all the great power of the wire rope and the metal sheeting that made the planes. She hit him without waiting, ran a closed fist hard above his eye, and he staggered at the force, both of them taken aback by the dreadful knock of bone on bone, but there was no turning. He put out an arm but found only the bare light hanging by its twill cord over the table so that the shadows around them began violently to duck and swing. In the tilting room he threw a hand at her and missed; she struck him again now with all the power of her frustrated worker's body, relieved happily of its forced idleness and inactivity, the power she had gained and earned in his lost war, and meeting again this power that had bested* him once already and had been besting him since, he crumpled there in the tiny kitchen and hit his head first on the table corner beneath the dizzying pendulum of the circling light, then raised himself only to slip backwards to the hard edge of the sink with a resonant crack, and the blows called out his weak, thin blood, whose compliant procession bathed him in the medium of his passing. The man her husband fell to the floor, and she followed him down. Between the table legs and the revolving shadows she watched bone heavy and opaque as he left through the fractures in his body, fractures put there by time and bad luck and finally her own machine-strong hand. She saw now what she had always understood before, but never in a manner physical and set and so pronounceable in words: that nothing could be taken unless something somewhere was also given in exchange.

All of this she accepted as part of the life that by the force of nothing more meaningful than chance was hers to accept as breathing was to be accepted if existence was to continue, as she had accepted the slaps of her sisters and the incomprehensible squirming of the boys in the alley and as later she would accept the man her husband's body pushing as others had with dry blunt unseeing discomfort into her, when his every part, it seemed, had the smell of gin, and its flavor, also, mixed with sweat and coal-dust and the stink of its burning, and beneath them all the faintest taste of urine. Other women in their whispering she knew dismissed what she willingly did as unnatural, but she saw further than they did, past nature to the part that man had built for himself in nature's clearings, the part to which she believed her disagreeable face and thick hands gave her access, the hidden places others couldn't share because they didn't see.

Thus she knew what the others would never have been able to perceive, let alone understand: that the man her husband with his hand raised had been a sign of acquiescence, of election, a signpost indicating the direction of the future and a switch to set it running, an admission that he would have lost his place, would need to lose it to save himself from further humiliation, when this last attempt at restoration had failed. The man at least had recognized the aptness of the coming departure, a thing that was ripe, and this readiness connected them, not as love connects things but the way that a face is connected with its reflection: a recognition and a fastening never sought but still not to be undone. It was his choice, she believed, but they would call it a crime, one to rouse every aspect of the great paperwork giant that was order and civilization. She imagined its huge movements, its fine scrutiny, saw the dull yellow eye of the creature open: from this, at least, if from nothing else ever again, she could protect him.

To consider this she did not need to move, or to stir in any way; instead she sat just where she had found herself across the room from him and let the day return through the high dirty window from the alley, press the shadows of the table legs across the humid floor now tacky with the signs of life expired, the slow dark lake of his mortality, then depart again.

Sometimes during this motionlessness she dreamed. Once she was walking through Trenton, but it had become a strange countryside, unfamiliar but not frightening, that she understood was somewhere near the front: the war was happening around her, she knew, although she couldn't see or hear it. Looking to a clearing between some trees in a forest of birch, she found the dismantled parts of the man her husband. She set about to reassemble him, but before the parts could be united the dream was broken, its beauty gone, and she was awake again with across the room from her the empty broken flatness of his inanimate shell, the dark incisions of his eyes floating across his face.

She could never tell how long she sat there, but eventually the ice in the box all had melted. The growing puddle mixed with the contents of the man's emptied veins and bowels; it wet her clothes. She took the sensation as a warning, and she rose. When next the landlord came to yell at them about the state of things, to call the man to shovel coal and clean the hallways, he'd have to find them gone—just two more luckless *people who disappeared into the funneling, endlessly multiplying complications of their own poverty. Now to step outside the apartment, cautiously to walk the building which from familiarity had become unseen and so needed to be encountered again: the door to the coal cellar was here, and another to the furnace room; there was a double hatchway cut by a daylight strip that led to the street. She considered carefully the stairwell that would take her to the front hallway, where lurked the unseen ones with their unseen jobs, porcelain-eyed and water-plain but present, and at the thought of their loitering turned instead to the furnace, shrouded in coal-dust and heat, where despite her resistance she discovered a resting place dusky with its own shadow, which, when opened, let a torrent of light in a dark world, a future into which the man her husband could disappear for the third and, she told herself, the last time, his lifeless body following the humanity and strength he had lost in Germany and the mindless instinct of breathing and eating and being animate that at last he had sacrificed to her fist.*

She waited a long time in the narrow passage for the delivery of an alien thought, something that wasn't this thing on which she had settled, but she was bound to her decision by the impotence of her poverty, had no other resources to muster than what the building itself could offer: this place and she were, for the moment, one, and though it took time to reconcile herself to the terror of her thought, to find her breath in the stifling air, at last she returned to the closed door of the apartment, one hand on the rattling knob and another on the jamb. She braced herself to work now on the unthinkable task as before she had braced herself for the unfamiliar singing mechanized danger of the wire-rope machines, knowing that eventually this, too, would be somehow accepted and unfrightening, that a dullness would settle and let her move through the worst of it without even noticing, that a numb new consciousness would be implanted, because that is the way in which life is able to proceed, and she trusted to the mechanism of life to see itself through.

Everything she had been so far disappeared in a way at that moment, was dispersed, and in the spectral steam of her evaporation she thought, For this there can be no forgiveness, even if she didn't know who it was that remained unforgiven, herself or the man her husband dead on the kitchen floor or the world at large. Then she opened the door finally, and passed through it into a welcome, bewildering daze. The opening to the furnace was too small, she knew, and too far off the ground, but of course it was only a matter of work, of setting herself the task and seeing it through.

She would be the strong one now, the one who would have to fight, to dig her fingers into the wall of indifference that faced them as the man had once done for them both, just as hers were the arms and hands that were strong with work, and the man her husband's had fallen into weakness, deciduous, as in a permanent winter. She would be both of them now.

It meant the sight in the watery glass the next morning was a strange one, but not somehow entirely unexpected: she, altered, not yet he, exactly, for that was a matter of more than clothing and hair, more than even the thick jaw and flat chest and strong hands—but already it looked convincing, even though of course there would be years spent forgetting the truth, the pattern of which would later fade so far as to be indecipherable from the whole, the past an era confused and indistinct. It required so little at first: the hair cut short and oiled with Wildroot, the soft-collared shirt, the legs of trousers, the man's coat.

Not so different was this figure in the mirror from the others who had left for war poor and come back poorer still in spirit and body, who were not part of the great new land that was to be built on the missing bodies of the dead, who no longer thronged around the factories or shuffled the breadlines. To the eye almost nothing worth noting—and yet she believed there would be this: that the many had been remaindered in the war's great division, rounded down and then casually set aside, while this new figure, alone, invented in their dying, was no less than a successor, fresh born and taking its first steps where they were tossing *down their last. It was clear from the mirror's face that no one would question or wonder. The transformation was inconceivable, and in this, too, it was a rebirth, bringing to life again the subversive and powerful spirit of the man her husband, his body spread now into the city, smoke and ash that joined the air and ground, one with the place and indivisible from it, and so she would remain with him here, in the city where he would reside in the dust and the dirt, in the soil and the water, where all of Trenton was his body, where the strength and freedom once his were retained, hers by bequest, something set carefully aside to be handed down, a tradition to accept at last as her own when all others had been lost. It belonged to the short hair and hard eye, the much-boned face in the mirror, to the vanishing woman who would be the man her husband's first and only son: something inherited by proximity of blood. It had taken only a suit, a pair of scissors, and the sharp knife from the kitchen.*

--- • ---

"Which one was it?" asked the tall one again. He took up almost the whole room, standing there looking down at the still man on the little cot-like bed. He was difficult to see: the lamp lay dark beside the overturned bedside table, and the bare bulb down the hallway pushed only a half shadow through the door. "Son of a bitch must have clocked him hard. He's out cold."

"He's breathing?" asked the heavy-set one from just outside the doorway.

"I'm not an idiot, Wade. I'd have told you if he wasn't breathing."

"I think it was that little fellow, kept his hat on, didn't talk to anybody," said Wade. "I saw them walk back here together. He left in a hurry, too, I saw."

"What 'little fellow'?" asked the tall one.

"There's no 'little fellow.' That's what I'm trying to tell you," said the one with the bloody nose. He started to stand up from his stool in the hall but Wade put a hand on his shoulder and pressed him down.

"Will you hold your horses for a minute, Al, Jesus. What did I say? Keep your head back, and pinch here. It won't stop otherwise." Al put his head back and pinched with one hand. With the other he wiped his handkerchief pointlessly over the blood caked under his nostrils and in the tiny cracks in the skin around his mouth. "Where's the goddamn light in here," Wade said, pushing his hand around along the wall inside the door. "Have you checked his eyes?"

"I can see from here, he still has his eyes."

"I mean are they rolled up in his head. Is he having a seizure or is he just out?"

"Here's the water," said the barman coming down the hall. Al, eyes on the ceiling and bloody handkerchief to his nose, had to turn his knees to let him pass. The barman handed the glass to Wade, who passed it to the tall one, who looked at it with discomfort.

"What do I do? I throw it on him?"

"No, no. For Christ's sake, you wet his lips. Didn't they teach you this in basic training? Just get out of my way, now, and will somebody find the goddamn light?" He took the handkerchief from his breast pocket and dipped a corner in the glass of water, then rubbed the wet corner across the lips of the man on the bed.

"We couldn't all be medics, Wade," said the tall one. "Somebody had to shoot at things from time to time during the war." Al started to chuckle but then said, "Ow," and stopped.

"I don't need to call the cops, do I? Or an ambulance?" the barman asked. The others responded with an expanding chorus of noise, and Al rose anxiously. Wade waved his handkerchief in the air. "Okay," said the barman. "I was just asking. Jesus. Guy's dead for all I know." He tucked his towel into his apron and left, and Al sat back down with a sigh.

"I should have asked him to bring a shot and a beer, too," Al said.

"I think he's coming around," said the tall one. "Who was it?" he asked loudly. "Was it that little guy?"

"I'm telling you," said Al, but Wade said, "For Christ's sake, will everyone be quiet, I can't hear myself think with all this yakking. And will someone find the goddamn light already, please, for the love of God? I need to check his eyes."

"Ah, nuts," said Al.

The tall one hitched up his pants legs and squatted down beside the lamp and the toppled bedside table. "Just unplugged," he said.

Wade slid part of a thigh onto the bed beside the unconscious man, who was now groaning. The light came on and the tall one righted the table and set the lamp there. Wade unclipped the shade and for a second they all shut their eyes.

"Don't move," Wade said to the man on the bed. "Now, look at me. Can you tell me your name?"

"You know my name."

"I'm not the one we're worried about. Now: can you tell me your name?"

"My name is George, goddamn it. What the hell happened?"

"Well, it looks like you hit your noggin pretty hard—or someone hit it for you. We were sort of hoping you could tell us. Look at my finger, and don't move your head. That's fine, yes. Good."

"Okay if I sit up?"

"I think so, but take it slowly."

George inched backwards until his shoulders rested on the wall behind him. "Say, is that water? Can I drink that?"

he asked about the glass Wade still held in his left hand. For a minute they watched him drink.

"How do you feel?" asked the tall one.

"Oh, copacetic," said George.

Wade said, "Do you remember what happened?"

"There was a guy, I hadn't seen him before. He didn't talk to anyone except to order his drink, I don't think. Just sort of hung back, like. I figured it was his first time, that he hadn't ever been, you know, with anyone before, or at least not around here, since I didn't recognize him. So I started to talk to him, but it was loud out there and he didn't seem to have much to say. Which is fine most of the time, you know. I felt as if he wasn't just being quiet, though, but like he was avoiding talking, if that makes sense. Then when he talked he was really hoarse, and I guess I figured that was why. Sounded like he had laryngitis, practically. Like it hurt."

"What did he say?"

"Nothing, really, just that he was fine, thanks, and no, he wasn't from out of town, and so on. Things like that."

"Okay."

"I felt sort of sorry for him, maybe. I said, Are you nervous, and he didn't say anything, just looked at me. His face never changed the whole time, now that I think of it: he looked at me just like that the whole time. I thought maybe he was just nervous."

"Sure," said Wade.

"Anyhow, I said something like, 'Let's go talk in the back' or something, and he said that would be fine, and we came back here. His face really didn't change at all. He didn't look scared or not scared, or excited or not excited. He just had this look, like he was thinking about something else the whole time. Even when he slugged Al."

"When was that?"

"A little later."

"When did he clock you?" asked the tall one.

"Just let him talk," said Wade.

"I know," said the tall one. "You need to read his brain waves with your pinkie, find out if he has meningitis. Meanwhile."

"All right, one thing at a time, smart guy. So you came back here. And then?" asked Wade.

"So, I figured the crowd made him jumpy, and then that voice of his, you could barely hear him out there by the bar. When we got back here, he didn't want to touch. I suppose I still thought that he was nervous, so I started asking him about himself, but he didn't really want to talk, either, or at least not about anything I could think of. After I tried a few things, where are you from and so on, he started acting like there was a problem. Then he kept sort of hinting at something. I got the impression he didn't want to be here."

"So why didn't he leave?"

George looked up at the tall one with a face confused for a moment and then shook his head gently, tenderly. "No, I mean he wanted us not to be here, me and him. I think he wanted me to go back to his place with him, although he wouldn't come right out and ask. Just said stuff about it being more comfortable at his apartment, having a bottle there of something fancy. Port? Something awful like that. I said we could start here, get to know each other a bit, then maybe some other time."

"Well?"

"That's when he started to get really weird. He started talking something about his wife."

"That's rich," called Al.

"Just keep your head back, Al, please. And pinch."

"I told him that wasn't my thing, couples, you know. Why get a woman involved—no offense, Al."

"None taken, I'm sure," said Al from the hallway.

"Well, he got really bent out of shape over it. Put his hat back on, talked about his fancy booze again, and at some point he said something like, 'I thought you people would do anything,' something like that. I guess that's about when Al came in, right before he said that or right after, I don't know exactly. I had left the door open a crack so the guy didn't feel pressured or trapped or anything, like to say all we're going to do is talk if that's what he wants. So Al comes right in and sits down next to him and the guy looks him over and says something weird to him. He says something like, 'I only need one.' "

"One what?" asked Wade.

"Right. That's just what I asked him. 'One what?' and he said, 'One of you people.' Or I think he said, 'One of you perverts.' Something like that, I don't know."

"Pansies," called Al. " 'I only need one of you pansies.' "

"Whatever it was, pansies or perverts, I saw it was trouble. I was done by then. I figured, 'To hell with this son of a bitch,' and I was about to get up to leave, but Al sort of went for the guy. I guess he was trying to be, I don't know . . . provocative or something?"

"I was drunk," said Al from the hallway. "I'm not any more, though, damn it all." With his wet handkerchief, Wade waved at him to be quiet. "Let him go on," Wade said.

"So anyway, Al grabbed for the guy's cock, and bang: without hardly waiting a second, he punched Al right in the face. I almost laughed it was so sudden. It was funny, too, in a way, because Al's the only one here I know of who's interested in women, so he brained the one guy who might ever have been up for it, you know, with his wife. Well, of course, I didn't know what in the hell to do, but I guess I stood up, maybe, and anyway that's all I remember."

"That's enough for me," said the tall one. "George is okay. If we leave now and each take a car, maybe we can find the guy."

"There's no guy," said Al.

"Oh, hell. Al's delirious. Did you check his eyes, too, while you were at it?"

"I'm not delirious. Will you listen?"

"Al," said the tall one, turning to the door, "would you give me a break. If there's no guy, who socked you? Sit down, please, and pinch your head back like Wade told you. Jesus."

"That's what I'm telling you," said Al, standing in the doorway. "Who socked me. I didn't know at first, but then I was really grabbing for it. I put my hand right down in there, really felt around, and that's when I knew. There is no little guy. There's a broad who's dressed like a man. A very strong goddamn broad in a drip-dry suit and an ugly goddamn tie." He sneezed suddenly, and the others all jumped as a chunk of half-dried blood burst from his left nostril, held to his face by a long finger of red mucus.

"Oh, Jesus, Al," said Wade, smoothing his tie, "put your head back. And pinch, I told you to pinch."

"Ah, hell," said Al, looking at his shirt. "It's too late anyway. This is ruined. Janice'll never get that out. It was new, too. I'm not ever going to hear the end of it."

Kunstler was out of breath and sweating hard, and an angry stitch dug into his ribs. He stopped running and turned around. The dark made it impossible to be sure, but through the muffle that was the noise of his breathing and his heart and the blood in his head it didn't sound like anyone was following. He rested his elbows on his half-bent knees and heaved for air. Running had left him wet through. The knuckles of his right hand hurt and were starting to swell. The bar had been hard to find, like a castle in a myth, but there was no going back: he was known now, an event fixed in their recalling, a thing that had happened and would be recounted and therefore remembered. Not that it had been working, anyhow. He would have to find another way.

The place was not exactly hidden, but it was not out in the open, either, and it was hard to find, but he figured now that he had expected as much. The first time he had gone too early, the noiseless hours of the afternoon, and it had been too empty, he had been too visible, had stayed to survey the place too long. Then he had been mistaken when he thought he could ask questions. In fact he should have kept his mouth shut, not said anything but simply nodded and paid, receded into forgetting, which is where he was safest. You should never question luck, he knew that, should have remembered it—and he had found the place, even the idea of it, absolutely by luck, carried there by talk in the locker room one day of somewhere not at all far from State Street being raided for "indecency."

"Right in the middle of town," Blackie said. "Can you believe that? It's in the papers, but I bet you won't hear it on the radio. They don't want to offend any delicate ears."

"What," said Bobby, "like a whorehouse?"

"Even the newspapers just call that prostitution," said Butler.

"So what, then?"

"You really don't know?" asked Blackie. "Youth today, am I right? They don't teach them nothing useful at school. When the newspapers say a place was raided for 'indecency,' see, it's always a cinch that what they mean is queers."

It was almost a year since Kunstler had first stood in the Parkside Avenue tunnel at Cadwalader Park, hours in the night's cold, a shoulder pressed to one of the stone pillars, worked the dodge of moving around it to avoid being picked out by passing headlights as they sliced into the walkway. The factory men sometimes told jokes about what was rumored to happen there, stories of acts glimpsed in passing, of men in pairs or groups, of bare buttocks pale between parted bushes. It was all too wild, of course, too exaggerated and elaborate to be believed, but there was always the hope that smoke meant fire. In his mind they were the furthest thing from himself that he could imagine: he thought of them as practically animals, insatiable, teetering at the very edge of self-control, as sure as an animal to eat any meat you put before them, and he imagined their dark joy in his willingness to bring them something fresh. When it was over they would share with him at least this: the terrible fear of disclosure. It would clad them all in safety.

.

At first the plan had just been the girl. For months every Saturday, and some Fridays, too, when he had money, Kunstler had climbed the poorly lit stairs to buy his tickets from the glass-caged seller on the landing. Then he would go stand in the long, narrow room among the wilted paper flowers and painted archways, the fading red-white-and-blue streamers. There along the walls loitered the Hungie cinder snaps from the foundries or the servicemen still waiting for their discharges, who would all willingly spend ten cents for hardly more than one hundred and twenty seconds rolled against one of the girls in the blanket of smoke and noise.

Sometimes he came alone, but often enough some of the factory others would be there, Jacks pulling hard on a cigarette rolled crooked and lip-wet, Bobby awkward in his church suit.

"Hey, Abe," Augie liked to joke. "How's your Napoleon complex?"—or something similar.

"Depends," rasped Kunstler. "You got a girl called Josephine?"

They always met outside. Here they would stand, four or five or more sister- and mother-darned blazers and loosely knotted ties and the tart carbolic odor of blue-collar clean on a half-lit street where drumming echoed recklessly from the buildings around. They waited as still as animals hunting or hunted, and when they moved it was with the suddenness of birds turning. If Kunstler found the others there, he waited while they waited, and when at last they went in he followed. He walked through the flaking beaverboard foyer as if going no place in particular, as if just off a train and trailing the crowd to the exit, eyes on the heels of the man preceding him, the movements automatic, carried by the machinery of their own progression. Once in the dance hall's rhythmic jostle the men jellied together in a slow, uncertain mass from which Kunstler dangled only slightly apart, his pockets full of his fists and a week's pay.

"Did you ever dance with that one?" Jacks asked, pointing to a bottle blonde. "She dances good. Real close."

"I don't think so."

"You really like that other one, don't you? Inez. You don't really dance with no one else."

"I suppose I like her well enough."

Jacks lowered his voice to what he clearly mistook for a whisper. "I thought you said she's a dipso."

Kunstler lit a cigarette. "You said she's a dipso, Jacks. I just corrected your grammar."

Inez was out on the floor with a boy of her own age, a boy weedy and pale and dressed in clothes too big for him, too long and too loose, as if they had been borrowed from his father. Kunstler recognized him as a regular. He and Jacks watched Inez guide him tripping around the room. Kunstler knew she liked to dance with this kid, with others like him, because he was scared of the girls, of how one of them might react if he started moving his hands down her back. Most of her customers were scared only of not getting their dime's worth of contact.

"I got to find a new job," she sometimes said when she had danced with someone particularly pushy. "This is for the birds." The other girls had admirers, "but I've just got you," she told Kunstler, and silently he congratulated himself that this at least had gone right, every gear in place. He was proud of how, on the night that Jacks had introduced them and Kunstler and the girl had shared their awkward first dance, he had escorted her right away to the long bar that filled one side of the dance hall. While they waited for their drinks she said, "Well would you look at that? The hem of my dress is coming undone. I repaired it myself twice already, but I always make such a mess of it. I hate to ask the other girls, and I really don't want to pay. God, I don't even like this dress any more, I've worn it so much. It's like a noise you're sick of hearing." She gave an uncomfortable giggle and shrugged.

Kunstler handed her the drink she had ordered, and before he had really thought about it, and even though he knew as if she had just come out and said so that what she wanted was someone to pay the seamstress, or better yet, to buy her a new dress, or even better still just give her the money in her hot little paw, and to hell with this dress and every other, he said, "I can fix it for you." The girl laughed then, loudly, rocked her chest forward and asked, "Of course I'll just have to take it off for you first?"—but when he didn't laugh back, just looked at her with that unchanging expression he wore, just sipped at his whiskey and soda and looked, she cocked her head at him and said, "Why, you aren't just trying to be funny, are you?"

"No," he said. "I can really fix it. Better than you did."

The girl put one hand on her hip and said, "You know, I bet you probably can. I bet you're one of those men who can do just about anything, aren't you?"

"I don't know about that," Kunstler replied. "I mostly just draw wire for the wire rope. But I guess I can fix your hem." The girl drank and laughed again. It sounded different.

He knew instinctively that the girl had to believe in fate, and understood why: the glancing blows of circumstance by which she had made her way seemed to call for it, a better and more comforting name than any other for how she should have to live. It tempered the struggle for existence. Kunstler counted on her trust in it, needed her to because to protect her was to make her unknowingly protect him, shield him from questions and uncertainties. This was the realm of her gift.

For Kunstler the matter of life was something else, and the great and real difference was this: that fate you would never need to work for, it came to you as if placed by a mysterious hand in the letter box—but this urge he felt was a challenge, a calling not just heard, but answered. It summoned the creative force in a man, who then constructed the world in which he succeeded or failed, constructed himself to suit that world, remade whatever yielded as he would have it. It was clear to him that of course many men missed their destinies, failed them through lack of action or of foresight, or through the very weakness they afterwards called fate when shortcoming left them passive and apologetic, but even to fail at destiny was better than the other way. To accept fate was to allow your least self to be maintained and not surpassed: destiny, the name he gave to life and living and the daily decision not to obliterate himself—that required something more.

Kunstler didn't dance with Inez much after the first month or two. His money was spent instead buying her drinks whenever the band knocked off for twenty minutes or if she didn't have a partner. The girl poured herself headlong into a recurrent boozy oblivion that to Kunstler was a guarantee of privacy, a vulnerability that bound and blinded her. When the time would come for the dance hall to close they always left together, the little man and his girl, and then she might ask him if he didn't want to go with her for a cocktail someplace. After that there would be the slow walk to his rooming house, the quiet search for signs of his landlord during which the girl would lean against the porch column and fight an urge to giggle, followed by the gentle shuffle that would piece by piece remove her clothes. She would lay beneath his hand on the bed and accept his clothed body beside her naked one, accept the probing fingers when to spoon was all she wanted and preferred, saying quietly in the morning as if in a gesture of faith and solidarity, as a vow that sealed their union, "I enjoyed last night." They wouldn't look at each other when she said it.

That first time she had gotten out of bed afterwards to find her dress basted and hanging from a hook on the back of the door. From the chair where he had half slept Kunstler watched her try unsuccessfully to wrap herself in the tangle of sheet so she could squat and examine the hem. He admired her bare back, the way it blossomed into the forked swell of her buttocks.

"Well, hey," she said, looking at the repair. "Now would you just look at that? I guess you really can do anything."

"Don't go spreading it around," Kunstler said.

At that moment, he had thought the girl would be enough. He wouldn't have been able to say when the change came, either—just that it had come, and one day the girl was not the plan, but only a part of the plan, a means to an end that he had maybe only just conceived, even if it felt as if he had been thinking of it all the time. He could pursue his desires, he learned, but not choose them. That was why it disturbed him that sometimes as he stood waiting for the wire to spool he thought of the girl Inez, of her lopsided smile. It sometimes seemed to him that nothing could be more dangerous.

.

He ordered Jacks to borrow a car from one of the factory men—a relic, Kunstler called it when it showed up. "Jesus, that's just fine," he said when Jacks pulled up. "Pre-war, but which war?" Jacks laughed his hard, toneless laugh at that until Kunstler almost regretted having said it. The three of them together drove with the girl's things in the rumble, and Kunstler's suitcase under their feet in the cab. The flat wasn't much bigger than where Kunstler lived before but it had its own kitchen and bath, and more privacy than any lodging house offered.

The super was a slim man with slack arms and a pale, bald head over which he pushed a slab of greasy hair. Kunstler said to him, "This is Jacks, he drove us. Don't worry, he's not staying. He has to take that car back before King Arthur notices it's gone. Don't you, Jacks?"

"That's right," said Jacks. "It's pre-war, but we don't know which."

"Your apartment," said the super to Kunstler. "Keep who you want, as long as they ain't noisy." He handed over a set of keys, which Kunstler handed to Jacks, who started pounding up the stairs with the girl's luggage, a case in each hand and another under his arm, the bags knocking against the balusters.

"Don't break the place, Jacks," Kunstler called. To the super he said, "I guess now you see why he'll be going."

"Sure," said the super.

"Sure," said Kunstler. "And this is Inez."

"Miss."

"Oh, not miss," said Kunstler. "She's my wife." There was a sudden silence on the stairway until Kunstler, his eyes never leaving the face of the super, called up, "Third floor, Jacks," and Jacks started walking again.

"Oh," said the super. "Of course. Well, then, Mrs. . . ."

Inez didn't speak, so Abe said, "Kunstler."

"Right," said the super. "Kunstler. Ma'am."

Kunstler shook the man's hand again. Then he picked up his bag, said to the girl, "After you," and driving her ahead of him, he walked up the stairs.

"Why did you tell him that?" whispered Inez as they climbed.

"What?"

"You know, about us. I could tell he didn't believe you."

"So?"

"So now he's going to tell everyone about how we aren't married." They stopped climbing for a moment, and Kunstler rested his case on the stairs.

"The hell we care. People are always trying to assign you some sin or another," said Kunstler. "I'd rather choose for myself which one I get than let a bunch of gossips pick it for me. It's like letting someone else pick your clothes for you, or tell you what position to sleep in. Anyway, don't you want to be married?"

"Well, yes, I guess so. Of course."

"To me?"

She looked at him hard and said, "Yes."

"There you go, then. Right down there: I pronounced us man and wife, by the power vested in me by my own god-damn self, with Jacks and that bald weasel as witnesses. So let's celebrate. Let's go on up and have a drink, and dance, and do whatever the hell else we want, because like he said, the place is ours."

"All right," the girl said. She began to cry a little, but smiled, too, and said, "Bald weasels be damned."

He watched her climb a few steps before lifting his bag to follow. He thought, *I am really hiding in plain view:* in the super's moist palm and weak disapproval he had all but disappeared, because no one ever thought to look past the first layer of sin to the next, past the shabby dressing to the wound beneath. The blind from which he looked out on the world was built of a wide-shouldered suit, of nails torn to the quick and too dirty to come clean, of Wildroot and aftershave, of the damp hand of the super when he shook it—but mostly of the girl, and he knew it. Her ringlessness was just more camouflage. Though it would hurt her when the neighbors reading her finger went out of their way to call her *Miss,* it made Kunstler feel not proud, exactly, but something like satisfied and assured to know of their awareness and condemnation, since he knew that their disapproval was also in some way indemnity, because from that condemnation they made deductions, and therefore thought they understood what he was: a man too selfish to wed the poor girl—practically a child—who shared his bed, a man of base appetites with a factory job and forty dollars a week that he chose to spend on liquor. A man to be judged in each case, certainly, but also in each case a man.

He knew for certain that day on the stairs that it was more than just the girl now, that he would want to complete the picture, return to the world what poverty and war had taken: the secret strength of the absent father, his raised hand a signpost, a switch to turn on the future, reconstructed in the son, what was silent in Kunstler to be spoken at last by another. Thus Kunstler would no longer be an angry spectator of the past: through the child he would have his revenge against time. This is how you cheat death; this is how you sail the slow, dark lake of mortality. This is how by means of the girl Inez he would manufacture the future and build a house for his name. One day, he foresaw, she would be drunker than ever, a swaying, bewildered drunk, and Kunstler would set her on the bed on her knees, open the concentric tubes of her girdle and dress and body, ready her for the waiting shadow and the plan which right that moment was taking shape in his mind, so that even as he quickly carried the girl, smiling in tearful pleasure, through the doorway of their new apartment, he was already thinking of the dark tunnel and the flesh between the parted bushes, the promise offered by the rustling grass; he was already on his way to Cadwalader Park.

When her father died at last it had been with all the windows open.
Afflicted by the petty thievery of mortality, he had loitered ill for months:
illness seated in his grimy hair and wispy beard, illness astride his con-
vulsing chest with its outdated clothes growing every day dingier and
larger, too, on his receding frame; illness spread cloudy across his eyes,
and her father aware, naturally, and not ignoring his bodily retreat but
neither really accepting it, never fighting or embracing the darkness to
come, an ambivalent prisoner attempting halfheartedly to appease his
captor. Without the will to battle his end or even the honor just to go, to
fold up and disappear, instead he would rot there in the midst of them,
shrinking apathetically inside the yoke of his celluloid collar and asking
always with his pitiful face for forgiveness. Meanwhile the household
shrank in keeping with his reduction, the furniture departing piece by
piece to pay for other things.

The doctor, who visited so briefly that he would barely withdraw
his shiny head from its hat, called always for fresh air in the sickroom—
called for nothing else, it seemed, before moving on, her mother towing
tearfully behind as far as the door. Towards the end snow sometimes
blew in, and her father had to be wrapped deep in blankets, all the few
they owned, so at night the girls slept near the coal fire in a worming,

hungry pile beneath their coats, and in the day they quietly crawled the streets of Trenton with a score of other children in the wake of the departing coal carts for whatever was left behind, as sooty with the will to live as the old man was pale with lingering and apathetic death.

They were made clean to go sit with him. The others he spoke to by name but to her he said, "My girl," as if to remind her what she was beneath the unsightly miscalculation of her features, even though the others called it doting and slapped her for it after. Later they would travel one last time into the sickroom with its few remaining pieces of dark furniture, the flotsam of their shipwrecked gentility, and the window not open any more but closed to retain the smell of poverty and death, all that remained alive of him.

•

Her mother's tearful despair was a thing she never felt. She sometimes believed it was because even then she had been ugly and known it, and the ugliness protected her from pain, or rather was a pain so great in itself that all others were small by comparison. It was impossible to remember, after all these years. She remembered the room, though, where the others cried, spread in a strange weeping arrangement amid the scattered, departing mahogany. On the floor just under the bed there had fallen a tasseled pillow, she remembered, and she knew as she looked at it that it was already a relic of the past, a dream, that it would disappear from her life and never be seen again, but the gold rope edge was so fine with all its twisted, fraying strands, that for just a moment she regretted it.

As the afterthought, as the others had called her, unformed and untrained (and in her blossoming still breastless and unbeautiful), she was left behind to help in her mother's work, which would consist of stitching clothes for other women, pumping the cast iron pedal in the ever-twilight until their heads ached and their legs cramped, or washing a household's sheets and linens in the alley behind. If they were lucky her mother would be allowed for a while to teach a girl the piano, which paid better and didn't try her eyes.

"You were born too late," her mother never ceased to remind her as they lay in the part of the small room they reserved by a curtain for their private affairs, sleep and the chamber pot. There had been days, she said, before his illness, not glorious but charming and lively, and full of comfortable ease, when they sang together in the evenings by a square piano in the little parlor; and her father had been a dapper man. At his passing the others all remembered and were driven to recollect it, but seeing how the memory hurt them she felt glad she had been too young to recall their brightest times. All she remembered was later, the bad days, when the other girls stole the food from her plate and warned her not to tell. It had been as if no father had ever watched her.

In the little curtained room she learned to baste and darn, to take the pinned clothes off a woman without pricking her, and to fold the clean linen before it was completely dry so it would take a sharp crease. Later in the alley where the washing was hung she learned other things, too, about the certain kind of young men who didn't care that her chest was flat and her lips hard and fleshless. She hadn't understood then their writhing insistence, but it was easy enough to satisfy and when it was done they would give her gifts, a swift gesture of transferral made without eye contact, without warmth.

·

That was how it was and would be with all men until the man her husband, and she submitted to it and to them because she understood the nature of exchange, without which for her everything was impossible, because until the war her sex meant she was never allowed to do any but the most meaningless work and so was condemned to poverty, which it seemed to her was as much a feature of her woman's form as any physical part. The only ladder meeting this wall of constraint was a man, so she traded the little she had, which was the still body beneath the one that bucked and jerked, and in return received as much or as little as these others were able or willing to offer her. If they were mindless fools whose fists she knew better than their faces or their eyes, if they remained as anonymous to her as a nameless puddle where you would drink only in the most desperate thirst, she accepted it because she understood this was to be the levy inflicted upon her by her natural lack of charm and attractiveness, by the weak body that was still never more than a woman's, however deficient in beauty.

These forgotten men never knew how far into them she saw, never suspected that in time it was far enough to understand that in their own ways they, too, were weak, weaker than she was who after all could endure the men and all the rest of it, and she learned there was a price weak men paid for the insufficiency each felt in a different way but all were condemned to experience. If this was no surprise to her, there was nevertheless something she hadn't expected: that to know these frustrations was in some sense at last to understand her mother and her grief, to see what it was for her to have found a man with some quality, whatever that might have been before he accepted to shrink and die in his soiled clothes of a gentleman, what it was for her to suffer the cruel chance once having found him to lose him again.

Thus she had known as she opened the door to the room that contained the furnace that whatever happened to the body of the man her husband, she would not easily accept to give up what in life he had been: someone who would never stoop to what was easiest but instead challenged himself to what was hardest, who was not afraid of fighting, audacious and confident enough to lie to anyone about anything when it was needed. For the benefit of them both he had without flinching fought and lied his way into a bare living all along the Jersey coast, holding jobs sometimes for a day, sometimes for a week or more, always telling people that whatever it was they needed doing, he could do it, whether pilot a barge or foal a horse. He was a man who, if things went wrong and they threatened to beat him, never ran but instead fought them back no matter what, because that was the way he remained the master of his own life and form and mind, even though afterwards he sometimes inched home bloodied and delirious from pain.

She knew that in what he did there was no sin, or rather that sin was only a name given to desperation by those who never felt it themselves, an idea to comfort them, to cool their blushing superiority. To her the man's lies were at worst predictions, wagers made in good faith against the future that sometimes he won and that, if lost, were accepted and then forgotten: the present was too urgent in those days to leave any space for the past. If sometimes when he was drunk he would slap her, it was not with the same impotent fury as the weak ones had done, who used the power they had—to protect her from absolute poverty, from the violence of even baser men—as a means of control. He offered her more than they ever had, too, for with no weakness to overcome he was free to share, and he willingly shared everything, since he didn't fear her: the booze he taught her to drink and the cigarettes he taught her to smoke, the food he worked for all over Trenton, or bartered, or when necessary stole, his room and his bed and the quiet, firm unspeaking in which he housed his strength.

Here was something not just to accept—as until then she had accepted the forgotten men and all the other painful necessities that constituted life—but to want, and to have it she would do whatever was needed, would move from one flophouse to another at a minute's notice when the bills came due, running quietly through dark streets with her few belongings tied in a piece of oilcloth under one arm, or care for him when he returned half broken from a failed ploy or a night spent drinking and fighting to relieve the frustration of helplessness that always threatened to settle on the heads of those who didn't take care to shake it off. All this was easily suffered just so long as they could be alone, for with him she found all she wanted, to be isolated from the world with the one person she trusted, to orbit him like a moon. She didn't need those other things women were expected to want, the accessories of domesticity, the meaningless kindnesses that were no more than gestures to their helplessness. The man her husband was the bridge she crossed, not from loneliness, which was a deformity of her bones, but from the terror of lonely suffering, and if the sensation she experienced in his presence was not exactly love, it was still and always something that she felt greatly, deeply, something even more than the astonishment and envy with which she at first regarded the flexibility he imposed on a whole world of rules, using them as vines use the spaces between the bricks in a wall. She admired him.

So when the moment came to face the terrible thing that had never been her own making but was the making instead of her ever-dying father and her grieving mother, and the man her husband's war, lost despite everything and in the face of public victory, and her own lot, which was ugliness and nature's darker part, and then the making also of the wire rope factory where her strength had grown to match the animal thickness of her brow and jaw, when she did away with the empty body that no longer contained him but worked mockingly on in his absence like a train whose driver has fallen from the locomotive, when later she opened the door to the whistle and dust of the furnace's dark burning, when she took up without looking at it the kitchen's sharp knife, she did it in the dawning and veiled awareness that this was but a passage, that even as the carapace disappeared, the true thing that had been the man her husband was liberated, freed to find its place and grow again within her, that soon within her he would be reborn.

_____   •   _____

He went to Cadwalader by car. It was because of the woman
on the bus, one of the half-dozen people there or more who
caught it with him at the same time almost every morning.
She wore everything up-to-the-minute, sweater-girl style—
and wore it all wrong, for his money. She was too skinny, for
one thing, and although Kunstler figured you didn't need a
second, she wasn't quite young enough for it, either. He didn't
like her sharp face: it was too pointy, it lacked flesh, promised nothing more welcoming than pencil-tip breasts, slatted
thighs, a bony wasteland. Thinking of her bullet bra, he said
to himself, *She has brought the wrong caliber gun.*

She had glanced at him a few times before on other days,
he had noticed, when they were sitting so they couldn't help
but see each other, sideways looks that she very nearly kept
to herself before turning back to her magazine. Today she
was right across, faced him over the swaying corridor of the
bus with her head tilted in such a way that her hat seemed
in danger of falling off, and he could see she was looking at
him without hiding it this time. Instead she wore an expression, one he assumed she had learned from the pictures or

the glossies: it was the one that said she was having a thought and, come hell or high water, she intended to share it. He almost expected her to raise a finger pensively to her chin. He would have read the news to cut her out, but reading on the bus made him sick, would cause the back of his throat to climb, so he left the newspaper folded in his pocket, and tried instead to look at nothing.

"Excuse me," she said. "Excuse me?"

He fought the urge to ignore her, and said only, "Yes."

She smiled. "Oh, excuse me. I hope you don't mind. Have we met? I was thinking that I'm sure we've met." Another woman looked over and smiled at them. Kunstler took a deep breath.

"We've been on the same bus pretty often, I guess. That must be what you're thinking."

"Oh, no. I mean, I know that, but I've thought all along that I must know you from somewhere else."

Kunstler looked away at nothing again and with a kind of desperation took the paper from his pocket, but there was nothing to be done with it, so he smacked it against his knee once or twice, then put it back. "I really don't think so," he said finally.

"This is so forward of me, I know, but you're from here? From Trenton, I mean—aren't you? I think maybe we lived down the block from each other." She smiled. More people were looking up from their papers and their shoes, Kunstler noticed, listening to her; he felt as if he were answering them all, along with all their colleagues and families and hairdressers and barbers, when he said, "Well, I'm sure you lived down the block from someone, of course, but I'm afraid it wasn't me."

"You seem very sure," she said.

"What I mean to say is, I only got to Trenton after the war."

"Oh. It must be my mistake, then. I'm sorry."

"No, that's quite all right."

For a moment the bus shook on; Kunstler and the woman and the others around who had been listening all assumed the unnatural poses of indifference that result from aborted moments of communion. They would make several more stops before hers, he knew, stops at which more people would get on than off. The bell rang and they slowed; there was a movement of passengers. Kunstler hoped for as many as could fit so one of them might come stand in the aisle and separate them, but no one did, or for an old lady who might accept his seat, but there wasn't one, and it was only once they were moving again that he finally thought of getting off. He was wondering if he should ring the bell when the girl leaned forward once more, and said, "But you do look so familiar. Might I ask your name?"

"Oh," he said, pressing a finger to his eye. "Sure. I'm Kunstler. Abe Kunstler." He crossed his arms as if he were cold, although in fact he was sweating lightly.

"Kunstler? Is that how you say it?"

"That's right, Kunstler." He moved a little in his seat, and began to bounce his leg a little on the ball of his foot.

"Abe?"

"Right." He was looking around now, eyeing the spaces between the others.

She smiled again. "For Abraham?"

"What? Oh, yes. For Abraham," he said. He found a handkerchief in his hip pocket and wiped his forehead. Then he took his paper out of his coat again, but a single look at it made him queasy, so he just slapped it against his bouncing thigh.

"Oh. Well, it's very nice to know you, Mr. Kunstler."

She reached out a grey-gloved hand between the standing men who held the straps. Kunstler put his paper away and took her hand in his and said, "Sure, fine." He was still holding it and looking at her when the bell rang again. He stood at the sound as if the bell were a part of him, part of the machinery that made him go, and said, "I hope you'll excuse me, Miss, but I just remembered that I, well." To the standing men who blocked the way to the door he said, "Pardon me," but only after he had pushed by.

He stood quite still for a long while after watching the bus pull away. Once he took his hat off. He turned it around a few times as if he were checking it for holes, although he didn't look at it. Then he put it on again. A moment later he pulled the paper from his pocket, only to stick it right back.

"Oh, that's fine," he said finally and pressed a hand to his temples. "Yes. That's just goddamn fine." He started walking. When the man at the Kaiser dealership asked him what it was he was looking for, exactly, Kunstler told him, "I guess I'm just done with taking the bus, is what it is."

"Well, sure," said the dealer. "That's junior-varsity stuff."

It was well past noon when they finished all the paperwork, so Kunstler gave up on the factory and drove home. It was the first day he'd missed on the floor since they gave him the job, and as the car rolled down the road he screamed in frustration until his voice shook.

Even as he thought of leaving, he knew he wouldn't: it was only here that for sure he could pull wire, he told himself, even though he knew without admitting it that pulling wire wasn't the only reason, if it was even the reason at all, that no matter what his job he would never leave Trenton, and it was because of the man, because it was only here he and the man could be together, it was only here that the man was in the smoke and the dust and the dirt, in the soil and the water. The man had been scattered and now all of Trenton was his body. He was from here and of here, one with the place and indivisible from it. So here is where Kunstler would stay. How else, he wondered, would the child be infused with the man's being? How else would the man be resuscitated into the world?

But Cadwalader Park was a long, slow bust. Kunstler knew almost the moment he got there that the tunnel would be a waste of time: practically all he saw were rich people in expensive new cars driving back and forth from places he didn't even bother trying to picture. He had parked some distance away and walked there along the wide, empty road, the white stone opening of the tunnel like a gateway to an ancient temple. Occasionally someone else walked through: a few times he saw a colored man leaving or going to work in one of the fancy houses on the park's far side, and once there was a hobo who, finding the place occupied, had asked for a cigarette in a tone of hurt surprise and when it was lit staggered away, leaving behind the heavy odor of soiled clothes. The few others who passed had stared at him with obvious suspicion. After a couple of Friday nights spent waiting around with no sign anything would ever possibly come of it, he started to worry someone would eventually notice and call the cops to report a man loitering half hidden near the kinds of houses men like him didn't enter except to fix a leak or make off with the silver. There was no option but to withdraw, he decided: the threat of discovery had crept too close. For a time he went walking through the park itself, but that proved no better: moving kept him warm, but away from the road everything was completely deserted and unnaturally dark, unnaturally quiet.

Next he had tried on the other side of town, out past the working districts near Hamilton, wandered and waited along Spring Lake and the marsh, with Deutzville and the world lit up just behind the trees. There were stories about what went on in the dark here, too, but for three nights in a row no one had walked by, not a single person. There were no rustlings or whispers, Kunstler saw no movement at all in the bulrushes. He would persist for some time, though, trying first one place, then another: this was the stirring Kunstler suffered, the strange tenderness mixed with ownership that the girl Inez evoked in him. It was against his better judgment but equally beyond his control, originating not in his will but his body, a creation that slipped increasingly from the command of its maker, so it wasn't until winter arrived in full force that he gave up, even if he had known long before the snow came that it was a bust. Then the factory others got to talking about the bar, and he knew that at last he had gotten lucky.

----------------------------   •   ----------------------------

It was almost spring when Kunstler put a match to a cigarette in an unlit doorway across the street from the raided bar near State and then subsided with the tiny chemical fire into darkness. He had a full pack, and he wasn't tired; alone and hidden he could be patient, he told himself, and he thought, *I expect some people won't read the news who ought to, or at least I hope they don't.* He was five cigarettes in on his third night when a man wearing a grey overcoat and wide-brimmed fedora tried the entrance. He found it locked, of course, and stopped for just a moment to look quickly around, then just as quickly he walked on, moving in the same direction as before. Kunstler threw his still-burning stub at the gutter and followed. They crossed East State, which glowed with thirty-foot-tall signs, all the places Kunstler knew the names of and never visited: F. W. Donnelly, Kaplan's, Reid's, the Savoy, S.P. Dunham. Although the man in the wide hat hadn't looked behind him even once since walking away from the locked door of the bar, Kunstler found the light unnerving: for a moment he instinctively hung back, as if fearful their shadows might react explosively if they were to cross.

A few blocks later the man turned east. On a street filled with businesses shuttered for the night he let himself into a two-tone Hudson. Kunstler continued to walk, came alongside the starting car. Through the window in the dark it seemed the man hadn't taken off his hat; either way there was no making out his face, Kunstler noticed, even as he reflected that there was no good reason he should want to. After that he walked cautiously as far as the freight yards before circling back through the emptiest streets he could find to his doorway hideout, where he stood smoking for another hour. He returned again the next night, and again the night after that, every evening after work for a few hours, he didn't know how many nights, until at last another man, a skinny guy in a campus jacket, tried the door. He stood before the vacant building longer than the other had, and looked at the door as if convinced it could tell him something. When he left, Kunstler followed him through a maze of dockside streets. Eventually they came to a different bar. Kunstler watched the guy go in, memorized the address, and then went home to wait for Saturday afternoon.

What surprised him most at first was that to look at, it was just a bar: if you forgot there were no windows and that even during daytime the place preserved a nocturnal darkness, if you ignored the curtained door at the back through which they sometimes passed in pairs or alone, then it was nothing so strange, a room full of men drinking beer and whiskey, the same smell of stale alcohol amid low lights, the same zinc and mirrors as a normal place full of normal people, the kind of bar he figured you would find just about anywhere there were people who worked and who afterwards wanted to drink. The barman, even the customers: they all looked normal.

"Not much business," Kunstler had said while ordering

his drink, and then asked, "It ever get full here?" When the barman only shrugged, he added, "Most joints get so full on Saturday, is all." He spoke clearly, not loud but easy enough to hear in the half-empty room; he realized suddenly that the factory floor had made him cocky. From his stool he could watch them in the mirror, three men talking, the barman twisting his towel, and across the counter from him two others, one customer in tweed and another wearing a charcoal suit and pearl-grey shirt. Kunstler found himself staring at that shirt, at the man in it. He understood already that it was too early, that he should have come at midnight, but somehow he couldn't yet bring himself to leave.

The tweed said something quietly to the others, shook his head. The grey shirt said, "What, is he writing a book?" and looked at the barman, who scratched behind his left ear with his right hand.

"Hell, I don't know," the barman said.

"Well, no one is going to drop any hairpins," said the one in the grey shirt to the tweed. Then to the barman he said, "Still, I suppose we should," and when the barman didn't move, he added, "And by 'we,' you know. I'm not the one who works here."

The barman slapped his towel against the sink edge a few times and said, "No, I guess not," before coming over to where Kunstler sat in contemplation of his empty glass. The barman worried the inside of his cheek with his tongue. "Anything else?"

"Maybe in a minute," Kunstler said in his rasp.

The barman nodded, ran his thumbnail along his jawline. "Well, okay." He glanced at the others. "I mean, I suppose. But I don't think there's anything for you here, see. If you just want to drink, hell. There's plenty of places." More confidentially he added, "People like their privacy, is the thing, and this is a spot, you know, for . . . for regulars."

"Members," called the tweed without looking up.

"Members, I mean. Right."

Kunstler was aware of the few others seated in the booths, although he couldn't see more than the tops of their heads or their hats hung from hooks between benches, and knew that they must have been aware suddenly in just the same blind way of him. Two men entered through the door at the back. The barman gave them a look and they stopped. Kunstler turned to look at them, too, where they stood awkwardly, and then slowly turned back to his glass.

"Members," he echoed back to the standing barman, who nodded.

"Yeah, it's a private place, you know. It would probably be better if you . . . well, you understand. This one is on the house. The next one is five bucks." He collected Kunstler's glass, left his money untouched, and walked back to the others.

Once past the door and the sound of a high laugh Kunstler pushed his hands down hard into his pockets and walked practically without seeing. For a long time his mind floated as if empty, but at the same time he knew that what it floated on was a thought: that if the place was full he could get lost among them, just another head in a dark sea of heads, another glass in another hand. Nobody bothers to pick out the one within the many if the one doesn't make a spectacle. He knew this already: if no one could see the whole figure of him it was simply because he stood so close. He was never more than details, the anonymous blur of a worker living in sin with his girl, who didn't talk when talk wasn't needed, who drank too much, was gruff and blue-collar, was boorish, was dull. That was how it should be done. This time he had done it all wrong, but there was still a chance, he decided, to do it right. He wouldn't make the same mistake twice.

It was almost midnight when several weeks later he tried the bar again. It seemed he was right—the man behind the bar didn't appear to know him at all. He ordered a beer and stood quietly, careful to draw no special attention to himself until the handsome one who called himself George had come over to talk, had invited him through the curtain at the back to the half-lit corridor of closed doors behind. For a moment it seemed as if everything was at last on track, that things had been set in motion, but again he had not imagined far enough: the man simply hadn't wanted to come away. Kunstler tried insisting, even though it was obvious his tenacity was as wasted as the time spent walking through the park in the cold.

"Oh, hey," said George. "Women, couples. I don't really do that." Kunstler felt as if he were staring at a wall: it hadn't occurred to him that there would be any question; he couldn't imagine one of them turning down a body any more than he would have imagined a dog turning down meat. "She's a beautiful girl," he found himself saying, vaguely. "We have a nice place."

"Sure. Listen, it's not a shove," George said. "I just don't, not with women . . . see?"

Kunstler would have left then, departed without trouble even though he was angry. He had put his hat back on, hadn't he? He would have got up quietly then and walked out, gone home and reconsidered, but the second one had to come in, had to grab him, and Kunstler recognized instantly that although this one was drunk, he nevertheless knew: he identified right away the surprise on the man's face, felt the searching movement of the hand around the athletic supporter.

It was the surprise Kunstler wanted to hit when he punched the groping man, watched him fall sideways off the bed where the three of them had been sitting. Then Kunstler was standing, and the one called George was standing, and Kunstler hit George with the side of the same fist, from which George's head retreated swiftly to the wall. Now George sprawled on the bed, deflated, and Kunstler stood looking down at him, and then the other man was beside him, blood from his nose crawling around his mouth to his chin and neck. The two of them stood together, looking down at George in silence, as if George were in charge and they were incapable of continuing without his direction. Lying there he looked like nothing more than a soaked rag draped thickly over a skeleton, and as they watched him Kunstler knew a breathless fear. In that fear he waited, empty of anything and everything else. Then at last George's chest rose and fell, and, accompanied by a grinding sound from his throat, rose again, and the other man was quietly saying, "Thank Christ, thank Christ." He was saying it still when he turned his bloody face to Kunstler.

The man seemed to realize just as Kunstler did that standing there he barred the way to the door, but Kunstler was faster to act: he took the man by the arm and swung him away, overturning the table beside the bed. The lamp fell and the room tilted into shadow. Kunstler ran from the darkness into the hollow light of the bulb's empty hallway and through that into the near dark of the bar, where he then walked—but quickly, head low—through the crowd of men. He had to ease his way through them, turn and dodge. One yelled at being bumped. "Don't go away angry!" said another. Then he was running into the night outside, with nothing in his mind but the blows he had struck, no movement through his thinking but of his fist to the yielding flesh, the thrust of his arm, the resonant crack of bone.

The next Monday morning before he left for work he sat on the end of his bed fixing his tie, and told the girl they didn't go out enough. "We need to have more fun," he said. "You want to go dancing? Let's go to some bars this weekend, dance like kids, drink ourselves stinky."

"Sure, baby." She smiled, and rolled back into sleep. He thought about it all the way to the factory: *I should have known that. I should have thought all along it would be the dancing.*

The dancing, but also the booze, and to make the plan work he led them both ever deeper into that hazy forgetful world, a confusing place where he experienced a strange mixture of ease and anxiety. It was the ease itself that caused him fear: to find himself in public with only a loose boozy hand on the lever of his self-control would make him jump, and he could grow furious at how often he caught himself with his guard down. Even among the factory others, who knew him and so accepted his chariness or at least were accustomed to it, he recognized there was always the potential for ruin. Drunken fights happened nearly every night in the factory bars, battles of pride and nerve among the workers, incomprehensible disputes among the Hungies and the Wops; the trigger for the next one was hardly ever more than two words away—and then eventually someone would think it was funny to pick on the little guy, particularly if he had a good-looking girl, a girl you might covet, whose thighs shook in her tight dress when she laughed, whose uneven mouth was an invitation to a warm world, and he knew of course it couldn't be one of them, never one of the factory men: no one they knew could be allowed to have even the slightest suspicion.

Kunstler himself came close on occasion to exchanging blows with the others, but with the closing of his fist he would recall the sound it would make against another man's skull, the knock of bone on bone, and that remembered echo brought him back to himself, caused him to retreat. Even contained, though, the violence was there, it was contagious, so even the girl would sometimes fill with it, brew her own quiet form of savagery, his hidden anger calling somehow to hers like a siren song until they would fight.

Once in their kitchen she threw her drink at him, but so weakly that she failed to break the tumbler. Kunstler picked it up from the floor. He checked for cracks and then wiped the outside with his palm. Then, standing in the puddle of gin and vermouth, he filled it again: more gin, more vermouth. He said, "Well," quietly, and then paused, and then put the refilled glass on the table in front of her again. He walked back to the bedroom and a moment later the girl Inez followed, and when she got there she called him a bastard and pounded him on the shoulder a few times and then hit him on the chest, which hurt more, until finally Kunstler pushed her to her bed where she stayed and cried.

In the kitchen he found her glass still on the table but empty. He filled it again and started back and on second thought turned to take the bottle, just the gin, which he drank straight while she sipped mournfully. Later she cried some more and he held her; then came the moment when she stripped and lay on her side, an offer to his hands although that wasn't what she preferred.

·

It couldn't have worked while the dance hall was still open. The girl was simply too unhappy there, and always on her guard, careful of the men who paid to grope her, the managers who were always breathing down her neck. They needed the money, so she wouldn't quit, but still she complained about it, the same gripes as ever: that the booze was watered, the band out of tune and lazy and on orders to play everything so fast that each song was a grinding trot. Worse than anything else was the other girls, who disliked her so much they stopped talking when she went to the powder room between sets.

They wouldn't change the subject, she told him, or pretend they hadn't been catting about her: she knew, and they knew, and to try to hide it was a lie they wouldn't go far enough to attempt. They just weren't going to let her hear the actual words. Instead, to the sound of the girl's urine hissing in the bowl and the muffled bar noise from past the beaverboard wall they struck matches and fixed their lipstick and slipped off shoes so they could massage their feet. As she left their voices started up again. She didn't complain, but at home he watched her through an eye half hidden in factory grime as she tried artlessly and with bravery to conjure the whole of custom by herself, the mysterious liturgy of female social interaction, gossip and laughter and knowing talk passed around in a coffeepot and divvied up with sugar tongs. This was how she would briefly conceive a whole and different existence, the kind she seemed to think belonged by rights to someone with a man and a home, a woman with hot running water and matched twins on layaway, who proudly bought doilies and aperitif glasses and flowered teacups with saucers. The thought of it erected in Kunstler a disgust that was also fear: he hated to think of her driven by this low ache to seek something not already contained in the apartment.

When the dance hall closed for good that year, Kunstler had worried that the girl would be forever and irretrievably finished with dancing, but in fact she never seemed to tire of it. It began the moment in the morning that Kunstler, washed and fully dressed, his face carefully and generously lathered, turned the short crescent grip of the lock and swept open the bathroom door to let the shower's steam escape. While he shaved, Inez brushed the previous night's gin from her teeth to the sound of the radio—jazz or swing, no dull symphonies conducted by some long-hair—and honored it in gestures concentrated to suit the space.

The radio came with them to the kitchen. The combined heat of summer and stove as she made breakfast would turn her slip into a clear cascade of sweaty cotton through which he could admire her soft white breasts and thighs, the rosy flowering of her nipples, the blue vein that rose to under her arm. Even seated across from him while he ate, her bare feet on one of the other chairs, she waved her hand to the music, choreographing the smoke from her cigarette.

It was there, in the dance she performed in the morning in their home, that Kunstler first perceived the beautiful complexity of it, as if someone had snatched away a panel to reveal the intricate pattern of cogs beneath: the advances and retreats, the range of motions, the fluidity, the relationship to the music. Seeing her dance later with the men he found for her, he was able to admire the control and skill, the command of the human machine. In every movement, in the angle of her head or wave of an arm, in every contraction and release of her body in the tight dress, the very flexing of her fingers, he saw operation, manipulation. Even her wildness, even her drunken rocking, was dexterity, a variant she cultivated, and he wondered at how unconscious it appeared, the spectacle of a bird in the air with no thought for the miracle of flight. Still it was a miracle he understood best in the reduced and limited dance she performed barefoot in the confines of their kitchen, a revision, a scaling, each gesture intentional, controlled, engineered. In the bars he was too distracted, maybe: always hunting for the right face, the right look. He stood at the bar and drank while she danced, his job to see to it she always had enough booze in her to be flirty, to giggle, to jump in a way that shook the meat in her thighs and made her eyes flash at the sound of the horns. The men all watched, and from within his blind, Kunstler watched them back, observing, judging, looking at them with the scrutiny of a breeder— but also through them, waiting for the one who would be the lens by which he could see the future.

To the enduring and perpetual dream of the factory he thus added this new vision, one that for the time had its own requirements, made its own demands in the form of long nights and music and alcohol. Just as his body and his will were one thing, the visions, the new and the old, both necessary now, were pieces ill fitted but nevertheless parts of the same engine, pieces that grated uncomfortably against one another in the mornings where their edges met. He knew this, of course, although maybe he didn't know just how dangerously they rubbed, how loud was the grinding of the gears as they fought to change speed, until the day Cowie, the new floor man, called to him, "Kunstler, over here," and when Kunstler nodded in recognition but kept working as if to finish what he had started, said, "Close that, come on," with a tone of almost satisfied aggravation in his voice, one in which the resentment of all the others that lay fallow but ready was present and eager.

Kunstler let fall the top on the stuffing box and without haste walked the ten feet to where Cowie stood. It was typical of him, Kunstler thought, to make someone walk over.

"You're working with no gloves now?" Cowie said. "What the hell is wrong with you?"

"Oh." Kunstler shrugged. He didn't even look down at his hands. There was a pause before he said, "Guess I forgot them. I'll go put them on now."

Cowie made a face. "Oh my Jesus, Abe. You stink of booze. Are you drunk?"

"I went out last night. I'm just sweating it off a bit."

The manager passed a hand over his heavy red face, then took the little man by the arm. Kunstler let Cowie lead him across the floor and through the far door into the concrete stairwell. Cowie held up a silencing finger, and threw a glance up the rising coil of stairs. He stood very close to Kunstler and without whispering, exactly, said in a small, hard voice, "You can't come in here like this, Abe. You'll get yourself killed. Worse, you'll get some other guy killed—me, with my luck. You have to go home."

"So I forgot my gloves, what's the problem? Come on." He made as if to walk back to the floor, but Cowie blocked him.

"No, come on nothing. I've looked the other way too much as it is. Yeah, that's right: I know you're hungover half the time. That's bad enough. Now you're drunk, because last night ended sometime this morning, right?" He moved his head around in a failed attempt to catch Kunstler's eyes. "You're going home, Abe."

"Bullshit. I'm fine. Get the hell off my back."

Cowie didn't raise his voice; instead he stepped closer to Kunstler so that their bodies were pressed together, leaning down so he could set his mouth hard to Kunstler's ear. "First, you're not fine, and second, screw you, you little fucking prick. I should report this. If I get caught letting you work in this condition, I'll lose my job. I don't know how the last guy ran things, but with me, showing up juiced on the floor is not okay." He eased away a little, and glanced up the stairs again. Then in a tone that was almost casual, he said, "If they found out I let you off without making a report, even if you only worked a goddamn minute in this condition, I'll be up a creek. You'd lose your job, too, by the way. So be grateful I'm not writing this all up, and punch out, Abe. Punch out right now." He moved over so Abe could get by. He said, "I'll look after your machine until this reel's through the blocks," but Kunstler didn't move.

"Don't be an asshole, Abe. You were in the army, right?" Cowie said. "Remember the army? It's just like that: I'm giving you an order. The order is, Go home. Go home and be happy I'll even consider letting you punch back in tomorrow."

Kunstler nodded. He punched out, and changed, not rushing, making sure to do it just the same as he would any day, although it took two tries to get his tie right. Of course Jacks had a lot of dumb questions when he saw Kunstler heading back towards the offices in his suit, but Kunstler said nothing, knowing Jacks would never dare to wander too far from his bucket while on the clock. From the factory Kunstler drove his car straight downtown to a bar. After having a drink to clear his head, he called Inez to come meet him, straightened his tie in the bottle-flocked mirror, and ordered another. *The hell with Cowie,* he thought. He'd figure it out. It was springtime. There was work to do. It was best to get started.

———————————————   ·   ———————————————

"Don't I know you?" the older man in the hound's-tooth asked. Kunstler's heart jumped sideways in his chest, but he didn't let himself move because just beside the man stood Inez with the other one, the stranger called Price, who was too right, too perfect, and—since for hours Kunstler had been feeding him booze—too expensive a prize to let slip. Giddy with happiness and a paycheck's worth of Kunstler's whiskey, Price had been dancing almost ceaselessly with Inez through the bar's violet smoke. Here perhaps was the one, the man he had been searching for. It was a chance from which Kunstler would not allow himself to be turned, so he took the other man's hand in a firm grip, sticky with the summer heat, and pumped it hard, and slapped the hound's-tooth shoulder.

"Know me?" said Kunstler. "Sure, you know me." He spoke the words just the way he had practiced in his imagination: his voice like metal filings loud but not too loud, accompanied by a broad smile and eyes forced wide. "Hell, everybody knows me—I'm the Lindbergh baby." The man laughed. Jacks and Inez laughed, too.

"Hey, you might be. It's been nagging at me since I walked in," said the man. "I feel so sure. I'm Joe Dixon, by the way."

"It doesn't ring a bell, but why don't you let me buy you a drink, anyway, just in case? Who knows, I might owe you one. Whiskey and soda?"

"Oh, well, then . . . Bourbon and water."

Kunstler told the barman and then leaned back against his stool. "So let's see now," he said to Dixon. "Where were you in forty-five?" He didn't listen to the answer. He was too busy watching the stranger Price talk to Inez, and Inez smiling, laughing at something he told her, too busy estimating how long it would take until they were ready, until he could leave with them for the safety of the apartment. He was sweating in the heat. Dixon was, too, but he didn't take off his jacket. That's how Kunstler had known right away he would have been the wrong type: anyone who wouldn't stand in a low-rent bar in his shirtsleeves in this weather was no good for what Kunstler needed, could never be a part of the plan no matter how drunk you got him. It didn't matter anyway, he thought. *I don't need any of these others if I can just get Price.* He said to Dixon, "I guess it wasn't there, then. How about thirty-eight?" He took out his handkerchief and wiped his forehead.

Dixon spoke again, something about the Pacific, and Kunstler nodded pensively, his mind still wrestling with his urgent, desperate desire for departure. Between glances at the girl he found himself looking again and again at the door. The barman came back. Kunstler put money on the counter and passed out the drinks and forced a big smile, forced it so hard he thought his jaw might crack under the strain. He said, "Oh, brother. I think I would remember being there, so I guess I wasn't. You went to college?"

"Oh yeah, you'd remember all right." Dixon laughed in a

way that wasn't quite funny. "College? Well, sure—after. On the bill. Kansas State."

"Wasn't that, then. I never set foot in Kansas. Or a college, truth be told, except to drop a girl off after a date, once or twice. Is that where you're from, Kansas? Where else might it have been?" Dixon told him places he had worked and lived, and Kunstler nodded from time to time and smiled, one eye on the prize, the plan he had engineered, the other on the exit. He bought another round; the machinery was running fine, it seemed, but Kunstler hated to leave anything at all to chance, and so made sure to lubricate the works now and again, just as he would again soon for Inez and Price.

"And that's when I moved back up here," said Dixon. "Maybe not the nicest city, specially when it gets this humid, but home is home, I suppose."

"Damn it," Kunstler said. "I don't know that I've ever visited any one of those places. Let me ask you something, Joe: Are you sure we even live in the same country?" They laughed again, and Kunstler lit them both cigarettes out of his shirt pocket.

He almost wished now that he could thank the girl from the bus. He had hated her at the time, had wanted to strike the inquiry from her face, grind the polite curious pointed questions into the dirt, but in fact she had helped him: Kunstler was never caught off guard by the same thing twice. He said to Dixon, "Well, I guess you didn't know me before, but you sure know me now, don't you?" and told him his name, the story of his being: *Abe Kunstler.*

While they shook hands again Kunstler looked Dixon in the face, really looked and for the first time that evening saw, absorbed, and it was a mistake, a terrible error, for he found or imagined he found or in his drunk panic forced himself to find hidden within the older features their earlier form, and thought, suddenly and against his will as if he were being carried head high by a mob, about an alleyway where washing was hung, and on the ground, one on top of the other, joined in a taut bucking, a writhing insistence, two people so young they were hardly more than children, and of something the boy gave the girl afterwards that each of them would have thought of and called not a wage but a gift. Hurtled into the memory and caught there as in a trap for a moment that rattled with terror, Kunstler wondered what it had been, the thing that passed between them, cupped his palm that had once been the palm of a girl in an alleyway in an attempt to imagine again the shape of it, but all he could conjure was the movement of the hands, *a gesture of transferral.* It wouldn't have stayed there long, whatever it was. Anything that wasn't already money went straight to the pawnbroker.

Kunstler's throat filled again with the desperate urge to push past the others and leave, a sensation that came from his gut and through it rose to the very top of his chest like a wave of vomit waiting in his stomach. He wanted only to take the girl and retreat to their apartment, or better yet drive screaming in the car, the voice within his throat as open and throbbing and impenetrable as the engine, the sharp white spur of the high beams cutting his path into the dark road at night, but just over Dixon's shoulder the one called Price was again dancing with Inez, who was drunk enough now that between bouts of joyful abandon her movements were sometimes hardly more than a gentle swaying. Kunstler watched the waving of her body in the music's underwater, the meaty promise of her thigh rocking as the stranger's palm skipped across it. He reminded himself what this might mean. He needed to concentrate, if only to tie the one knot in the rope that would let him climb, and so he fought the sudden impulse that was almost a longing to reach into Dixon's face and beat the younger self from it with his fists. Instead he forced himself to think of all the bars they had visited, all the men, if they were even old enough to be called men, who he had met and loaded with booze and hints, the few that he had even gotten as far as the bar door before they sensed somehow the terrible inflexibility of his desire and recoiled. Kunstler felt hot. "But this time, maybe," he said in a breathless quiet.

Dixon asked, "What was that?"

"Oh, nothing," said Kunstler, surprised to find he had spoken out loud. He shook Joe Dixon's hand again, a sweaty, nervous, angry shake this time, and manufactured for him again the same smile, trying hard not to think or recall so the panic and the impulse shouldn't rise further, shouldn't grow in his chest and explode into violence. "Well, I suppose it's nice to have met you finally after all these years of missing each other in Kansas and the Pacific and where the hell ever. I need to go talk to my friends, but say—do you know Jacks?"

Even as he made the introduction he desperately acknowledged that the threat was not defused, not ever really deactivated, just postponed perhaps, or simply ignored as it ticked away the time until everything might fall apart if he wasn't careful every minute. Kunstler forced himself to think of the plan, the closeness of his desires after so many failed attempts, the reason to stay, and so he thought it, told himself again, this time in a kind of terrified satisfaction: *Yes, I should have known that. I should have known it would be the dancing.*

Kunstler turned to the bar and ordered the next dose of encouragement: gin for the girl, straight scotch for himself, soda and ice for the stranger. Kunstler drank most of his fast, unable to stop himself. He would be armored against compunction and indecision, he would be numb to all distraction; nothing must get in the way. He already knew that she would complain about the taste of the straight gin, that he would have to convince her to drink it anyway. "Better make me a gin and Italian, too," he told the barman. "I'll be back for it in a minute." He dropped money on the bar, tipped the last of his scotch into the glass of soda he had ordered for Price, and set out across the dance floor.

The girl Inez was deeply drunk now, a disoriented, lurching drunk in which Kunstler hoped she would be lost to a world as much imagined as perceived, her thoughts hooded and obscure, so that he and the room—and with them, the waiting shadow and his plan—might be reduced to the silhouette of a pliant and forgiving dream, and he hoped that if in the morning she remembered it at all, it would be so strained and distant she could still coyly say, "I enjoyed last night," that fixed and invariable oration that was her blessing and her pardon, granting clemency and absolution and confirming again the grand, unspoken entente that guided them—the one by which she was his and he, in his own way, hers. They wouldn't look at each other when she said it.

Kunstler had only been able to hope he was timing the drinks right. It was important to arrange it just so: if the girl would need to be lost in herself, whirling and away, the stranger had to be brought to a point of forgetful compliance without wilting past it into uselessness. Sometimes he had taken the men too far, left them vomiting in restrooms or passed out on vinyl booth seats.

Inez almost spit on him. "Oh, hey, Abe," she said. "Why, that's just straight gin."

"Is it? I guess the guy didn't hear. I'll get you a right one, but I paid for that, you might as well drink it. Go on, drink up, give me the glass back. How's yours?" he said to Price.

"Swell." Price smiled gently. "Although in fact, it's a bit weak, really." Kunstler sniffed the glass of soda water and ice and made a face. "Call a drink like that weak, means you've had enough, I guess," he said.

"You're probably right. I sure know I'm feeling it." He spoke with a loose-necked movement, his eyes dark incisions afloat on the pale sea of his face.

"Gee, I hate it straight," Inez said. She handed her empty glass to Kunstler so clumsily she nearly dropped it.

"I'll get you something good to wash it down." He returned quickly with the waiting cocktail, and stood by as she first tasted it carefully, then swallowed a mouthful. "Better?" he asked her.

"Yes, better. Better, butter." She laughed. "Better, butter think I'm drunk."

"You want to make something of it?" Kunstler asked.

"You're poking fun now."

"Sure," said Kunstler. She started to slip a little then, a slight spin and a slide towards the floor. Kunstler caught her by the elbow, sticky with sweet vermouth, and guided her to a chair. To Price he said, "I think maybe we had better help her to get home."

"Oh, you two aren't? I mean, I thought maybe."

"Maybe what?"

"Maybe you two. And that then, I suppose I thought maybe you'd try to sock me." He gave a little laugh. "Because, you know, sometimes when we were dancing, see? Gee whiz." He drank some more.

"I get you. Let's take her home. It's not safe for her walking around like this."

"Because sometimes when we were dancing, you know, and, oh brother—I sure don't want any trouble."

"That's right, no trouble. Take her other arm," he instructed Price, but it was Kunstler who eased the two of them into the backseat of the car.

Steering them through the hot summer-night streets, Kunstler realized that he was drunker than he had intended. From the backseat of the car the stream of Price's voice rose sometimes above the buzzing rush of the engine, but from what Kunstler could see in the mirror Inez slept through whatever he was saying. She roused enough when they were parked to get out by herself, mostly, and to say, "Well, well," a few times while Kunstler led them to the door of their building.

He had Price help Inez most of the way up to their landing, following close behind them in case one or the other should slip. He sat Inez on the stairs while he snapped open the lock, turned on a light, and shepherded Price to the seat in the small foyer. Getting Inez back up again was a job, and in the end Kunstler had to lift her. It was not like before: her body now was heavy and disobliging, her head rolling, unpredictable. He made his way carefully into the apartment and thought to himself, *This is the second time I have carried her through this doorway, I guess we must be good and married now.*

In the bedroom he laid her on her stomach. He was aware how much he wanted her. Even as he helped her find the pillow of her bed and his design took shape, as he removed her shoes and started to unhook her stockings, it had the power to distract him: the thick spill of her thigh in its nylon, the promise that swung with her breasts, the irregular upper lip sweeping through the rupture of her mouth. He thought of her saying that spooning was her favorite part, but insisting that he shouldn't worry, that she liked the rest well enough after something to drink. There was plenty of drink in her now; he had seen to that.

Back in the living room, Price was asleep. The apartment door hung open to the landing and the stairs, the looping funnel through the building to the world outside. Kunstler carefully closed the door, and locked it, then stood looking down at the sleeping man.

In Price's face Kunstler saw something of the man whose name was now his own name, the man who had been lost to the war and the kitchen and the furnace, a resemblance both desired and somehow insufferable. Kunstler had to fight an urge to cup that face in his hands, had to focus instead on the thing that would follow, the pale shadow, the thrust of the human limb, the coalescence of all his plotting into a moment of action. He would do this because he understood what the girl didn't: that it wasn't people they needed, certainly at least not the people they could meet, who would be forever detached from them and so a threat. Rather it was someone of their own that was called for—someone like them, someone of them and for them, someone who couldn't be lost but was irreversibly and conclusively theirs, a rebirth of the man from themselves, that they could share him, that he would be theirs alone.

This thing, this indefinite capacity, was in him. It was the engine of his progress, had been the figure pointing the way, a signpost indicating the direction of the future, a switch waiting to be flipped. He had responded with all the power of his worker's arms, the factory resident within him, lashing out instinctively, without thought, without intention, and released from the man the slow dark lake, and with it his inheritance, the thing he would become. In that moment he had been reborn and thus born, a gift, and he would repay it to the man who reposed in him, for whom he was the very tomb from which to rise, for whom the blue-edged bandages pinned around his chest were the half-open shroud. He ran his hand along the downy face and Price opened his eyes.

"Oh, well hey, mister," Price said. "Are we there yet?"

"She wants to see you," said Kunstler in his hoarse little voice like a crushed tin can.

"Is that right?" Price offered a diffuse smile. "Honest Injun?" He made a motion to get up.

"You need a hand, there?"

"I'm just jake," he said, but accepted Kunstler's help. Kunstler pushed him slowly down the short hall, and sat him next to where Inez was lying on the bed. "Daddy's home," Price said. "Time to get up." He closed his eyes and swayed.

Kunstler wiped his forehead on his sleeve and set to work. First he tried to raise the girl onto her knees, but she was caught somehow on the skirt of her dress and in the semi-dark he couldn't figure out where exactly it was holding. Kunstler said *God damn it* under his breath. He got up and walked around to the bed's other side, where he had space to lean forward and grip the hem. He pulled hard, so the whole thing wadded around her waist. The jerking shook the mattress, and Price began to topple.

"Oh, shit," said Kunstler. He said it again and again, *shit shit shit shit shit,* as he ran all the way around the bed to catch the sagging form that slipped gently sideways towards the floor. He righted the falling man and gave his shoulders a light shake. "Hey, there, brother. Hey, buddy," he said. Price came around with a start, and said, "Oops."

The summer heat was oppressive in the bedroom, and Kunstler had sweat completely through his shirt. He didn't want the windows open, as he intended to keep whatever sounds they made to themselves, but now he had to keep blinking hard to keep the salty drops from stinging his eyes. Holding Price with first one hand and then the other, he tried to shake off his jacket, but the right side caught on his shirt-cuff button and wouldn't come loose. For a moment he stood, left hand holding Price by the top of his head, right hand trapped in a long trail of inverted coat sleeve, frustration rising in his chest. "For the love of Christ," he said out loud. He put one foot on the bed, and rested Price's face against the inside of his lifted thigh. The jacket he removed roughly with his free left hand and threw across the room. In a fake British accent, Price said, "Steady there, old man," and then in a kind of singsong, "I'm Manson Price, sir, and I'd like to speak to the captain of this ship."

Kunstler settled Price back against the headboard. This time Inez was supple and frce, and he was easily able to fold her at the waist and arrange her knees apart. He looked at her for a moment, the cleft of her body rent and exposed. With a mouth-wet finger he began to part the tangled hair between her legs. She made a small noise, a sort of mewing in her throat, and Kunstler whispered tenderly to her that she shouldn't worry. "You just have to be ready, is all, and then it will be just fine." He rested his face against her leg while he worked on her, and breathed in the smell. The girl soon started to press back against his fingers, which now slid easily. The room felt incredibly hot, and Kunstler wiped his brow against his shoulder.

Kunstler went to Price and gave the man a shake and a light slap. "Don't pass out," he said quietly, almost desperately. "Just don't pass out on me."

"Excuse me," Price said without opening his eyes, "but have we met?"

"Time to get to work," Kunstler told him. He undid Price's belt and fly and tugged the pants out from under him so they fell to his ankles. "Come on, friend," he said. "Daddy's home, remember? Time to get to work. Come on."

"What's the rush, Skipper?"

"It's Inez," Kunstler said gently. "She's waiting for you. Are you going to keep her waiting?"

"I certainly ain't."

"No, you're not, are you?"

"No. No, I certainly not, am I ain't," Price said. "Although." His face folded then into a sad smile and he sighed.

"Sure," Kunstler told him. "Don't worry, we're going to fix it. Everything is going to be just right."

"Daddy's home."

"That's right. Now, let's go, brother. It's time to get to work."

Walking was difficult for Price with his pants down around his ankles and even over the short distance from the headboard to the foot of the bed he nearly fell twice. Kunstler stood him behind Inez and pulled down his shorts, but he could see Price wasn't ready.

He took Price's hand and ran it along the cleft between Inez's open legs. He pressed his mouth right to the man's ear, and asked him, "Do you feel that?"

"I . . . yes," breathed the other. Their hands together were getting slick.

"You feel it? Yes? Do you want that?"

Price inhaled deeply. "I plead Fifth," he said, but accepted Kunstler's slippery finger gently into his mouth.

"You recognize that, right? You want it, right? Yes? Don't you? Good. That's good. Okay, let's see if you're ready for it. Let's see if you can do your bit, here, all right?"

"Yes," said Price again. "What the hell, I might as well."

With his scented palm Kunstler gently brushed Price's cheek, only a little rougher than his own, and then suddenly kissed him at the corner of his mouth.

"Well hey," said Price.

"The good stuff is coming," Kunstler told him. "You just have to be ready for it." Price's eyes were still so heavy they barely opened, Kunstler could see, but he was getting hard now. Kunstler spit in his palm and then held it out to Price.

"Spit in my hand there. Go on, spit in my hand, now, like we're making a deal." Price let a wad of saliva fall down his chin. Kunstler ran his wet fingers around Price's cock. He kissed him again, this time fully, his tongue inside the other's mouth, straddling the man's thigh and riding it in terse jerking movements. He slipped around behind him and pushed him a short shuffling step forward until he was right against the kneeling Inez, and then guided him inside her. Price was only moving slowly, so Kunstler slid his wet finger into him from behind, and like that the three of them rocked back and forth until Price stiffened into a noise.

.

Price had passed out, so getting him dressed and on his feet again was hell. He threatened to vomit twice on the way to the living room. When they finally reached the landing Kunstler held Price up by the lapels. "You okay there?" he asked.

"I'm tired," Price said. "Serious, I just need lie down, if that's enough with everyone. I don't need fancy, understand. Just floor will do."

"Not yet. You can sleep later, when you get home."

"I'm sure that's right. But, I'm the floor, you know. And is this trip really necessary?"

Kunstler looked down the stairs for a moment, and tightened his grip on the man's jacket. He thought briefly of a slow dark lake of blood from a man's head, of a fist against a face and a body falling to the floor, meat heavy on unhinged bone, a heap at the bottom of the stairs; then he looked through these thoughts to the face of the drunken Price.

"Hey," Kunstler said. He gave him a light slap on the cheek. Suddenly he asked, "Buddy, hey. How old are you?"

"I'm, my take Fifth," Price mumbled. "The grounds that incriminate me."

"No, come on. How old? Nineteen? Twenty?"

Price nodded. "Nine ten," he said.

"Jesus Christ," said Kunstler.

"Don't get sore, mister, it ain't my fault. And don't take it wrong, I know. Sometimes when we were dancing, see, and the thing is, I think your friends in there liked me. I sure liked them."

"I guess they liked you fine. But now it's time for you to go," Kunstler told him.

Price nodded again. "Just a rest, pal, little bit." He made as if to sit, but Kunstler held him up, and Price had no strength to struggle.

"No. You have to go. Got it?"

The young man nodded. "Into sunset." Kunstler pointed him at the stairs, but it was clear that he would never make it down on his own, so together they trundled slowly to the lobby. Just before Kunstler let Price out the front door, the young man leaned into him and said in a voice conspiratorial and sly, "Less and another."

"What?" said Kunstler.

"Less you me go, have a other drink."

"No," said Kunstler. "No more drinks. You have to get out of here."

"I know, I know, but wait," said Price, his face crumpled with concern. "What about that, mister? Huh? How about 'em?" he whispered.

"How about what?"

Price looked at him with something like concern, an almost tender gaze, and in a voice filled with the happiness of promise, he whispered, "Waffles. Mister, how about waffles?"

Kunstler kneed the door open and gave Price a push, watched him reel as far as the next building. Then he looked around the tiny lobby, as if he worried someone else might be there undetected. After a deep breath, he went back up the stairs to Inez.

The girl was still folded at the bed's end, her legs forked, her face flattened into the sheets, one foot starting to travel towards the floor. Her bare thigh caught the light from the hallway. Her mouth was open and her breathing came rough and loud. Kunstler rolled her on her side and rearranged her legs. "You should put your knees up to your chest, now, like this," he said to her. "I heard somewhere it works better that way." He lay down beside her, and put an arm around to hold her in position. "See," he whispered. "Now we're spooning. Just the way you like." He wondered how many times they would have to try before it worked.

part two

1971

——————————— * ———————————

Kunstler would have to go looking for him. There was no choice. For two sleepless days he had missed work so that the boy's mother wouldn't be alone in the apartment for the boy to come back to, keeping watch the whole time from the seat that let him lean out of the kitchen to see the front door. He had to keep them apart, at least until he found a way to deal with the boy. Now that she was finally going back to her job, he could go out and search. There was no other choice, even if he didn't have an idea where, even if he hadn't thought yet what he would do when he found him.

But that's not true, either, he told himself. In fact, he had thought about all sorts of things—if thinking was the right word for the flashing, spectral images. He had even thought that he might kill the boy, although his imagination never offered a view of the death itself, only a suggestion of the still, recumbent body, unmarked, immaculate except for the wound he had been born with, the twisted ball of his face, until at last in this strange, gathering vision, while the boy lay as if the spirit had passed of its own accord, the abdication of living a gift, an act of filial piety, sparing Kunstler the sounds of death, the slow, dark lake of blood, even the boy's face was finally washed clean of disfigurement, in its place a soft nothingness.

He had imagined, too, that he might just stand there and make the boy say it again, shake him, beat him if necessary, until he said the words. He wanted to hear him say them so often and so loud that at least there could be no doubt, and then keep saying them until they lost their meaning, until he lost the ability to speak, until time ended or they both died. He told himself that for every problem in the past there had been a solution, that his safety had always been his own doing and no one else's, and so it would be this time. The boy was young, a child: he could be convinced, dissuaded, threatened. He could be beaten until he knew nothing for sure except that Abe Kunstler was a man. Kunstler tried with eyes closed to see the moment in the future when he made this happen, but he couldn't. For one shocking instant he saw the past instead: the face of the man as he fell to the floor of the basement kitchen.

The missing fingers on his right hand started to hurt. Wherever they had ended up, rotting in a garbage can behind the factory, or probably buried in dirt and pathetic sentimentality somewhere by that idiot Jacks and decayed since to nothing, they were throbbing now. Would knowing where they were make the pain less? He let his eyes close, but gave his head a shake: he refused to imagine pleading with the boy, or with anyone. He wouldn't beg. What was there even to beg for? He would tell the boy his mother was dead and then throw the ungrateful little intruder out in the street. Then he would come home, where he would tell the mother the same: that the boy was dead, that there was nothing to be done. He would be there when she cried over it, the child lost too late, a drink offered to soften the blow. *A ceremony,* he called it in his mind.

A ceremony: he imagined Jacks in the factory parking lot with a priest and a Bible and a tiny satin-lined box for the remains of his fingers, the liturgy, the committal performed in miniature, the priest a doll leading a toy hearse, all in keeping with the relative size of the deceased—which was also the size of Jacks' brain, that sap. It almost made Kunstler laugh to think of it. He couldn't ever understand why the boy's mother was so committed to the oversized fool, and always had been, even in the days when they had worked together in the factory, and Jacks to her, and to the boy, all of them together. Jacks the moronic janitor with his rolling bucket and mop like a housewife, Kunstler working the coils and capstans: the old days, now missed, when Kunstler had gone out every morning to yell his voice into existence. He hadn't needed to do that in years. The effect was fixed at last, his voice his own, one thing that didn't need to be constructed daily, just as once the bleeding had finally stopped a few years ago he had no longer needed to keep hidden from the girl that he shared with her the container of Modess wool tampons under the sink, carefully refilling them from a box stored behind the service panel under the bath. Maybe it was these changes that had made him forgetful, he thought, encouraged him to grow careless. Had the falling away of the routines he didn't need led him into complacency? He hardly even shaved any more. He would go back to it, he promised, go back to them all: *I will be myself again,* he told himself, thinking of a young, hard-boned face in a mirror in the basement all those years ago, and again he caught an image of the man, dead, but he forced himself awake and blinked it hard away. Awake or asleep, these days he dreamed always of the man.

Inez was there. "I'm leaving now," she said. Kunstler, belt undone, short-sleeved shirt unbuttoned and undershirt showing the ragged blue edge of his bandage, looked up at her from his seat at the tiny table. Circles of sweat already fouled his polyester underarms. "Are you working today?" she asked. She turned to the clock that ticked on the little counter. "But you don't start for hours. Why are you up already?" She stood looking in through the door to the kitchen, still an alley, the same space with the same dimensions in a building that was different but not different enough, the stairway still a mountainside, the tiny bedroom filled still with the same twin beds, which time had left hammocked and lame. Nothing was new or fresh, no veneer was intact: the linoleum had worn through to the wood, the enamel on the sink retreated from the black iron below. The paint and plaster fell away from the walls and the ceilings and the windows rattled in frames they no longer fit. Even if she never said a word about it, he knew she was disappointed. He could smell it on her. He didn't move.

Inez roused him with a hand on his shoulder. "Look at you, you're barely awake. Did you sleep any at all?" she asked—but he noticed that as she said it she didn't really look at him.

"Maybe," he said, running his good hand over his face, pushing the sweat down to his jaw. It was as if he had only just then remembered the heat. "Who knows." He picked up his open pack of cigarettes from the table but didn't take one. He stood.

"So stay, Abe. Rest." She briefly put her open palm near his face but didn't touch him. "Your fingers hurt? From the humidity?"

"Even if they do, I still have to go," he said.

"I'm taking an extra shift this week," she said. "A late shift, time and a half. We can afford a day off for you."

He shook his head. "No, I have to go. I missed too many days already. They're getting pissed off with me upstairs, and I can't say that I blame them, even if they are filthy son of a bitches."

She nodded, and then asked quietly, "Is Art still off with his friends?"

"Sure," he said. "He's running around with some of those hippie kids."

"Did he call? Did he give you a number?"

Abe looked at his cigarettes again. "I could barely hear him. They were somewhere, a party. It was loud."

"When did he call?"

"Summertime is all one big party, no day, no night. The kids now don't work when they have time away from school the way we did, they hang around and listen to that music. He should be working now. A summer job, teach him some responsibility, not running around all the time." Inez nodded again. He knew she wouldn't argue with him. She never argued with him any more. He wasn't even sure if she knew or not that he was lying.

"You want some help with your shirt buttons?"

"Don't do that," he yelled. "Don't start again with your goddamn coddling. Jesus, that's what, that's what—" He couldn't finish. He shook his head in silent anger as he swung past her and down the short, dark hallway towards the bedroom, his empty belt buckle clicking as he moved, his breathing loud.

Inez walked to the front door and snapped open the locks. She had left the chain unhooked in case Art came home. For a moment they were both quiet, then almost in a whisper she said, "Maybe . . ." but she seemed to change her mind. Putting on a hard, bright voice, she said instead, "Maybe make Jimmy drive. You can get some rest that way."

Kunstler leaned a shoulder against the wall, his body motionless except the hurdled suction of his breathing. With a claw of thumb and ring finger he began to pick a cigarette from the crumpled pack, but let it drop back. Finally he said, "Driving's my job. Where the hell did I leave my shoes?" Once he heard the front door shut he took the old sales receipt out of his hip pocket and read it again: *Rudy's Record Store. Item . . . $5.98.* The slip was more than two years old, but it was the only thing in the boy's room he had found so far with an address on it. The boy had used it as a bookmark. It was ridiculous that a child who had never worked a job had money to spend on things like this, could afford to buy himself trinkets and garbage. Wasn't it a sign of the life Kunstler had given him, this invader who had stolen the place, the life, intended for someone else, for a strong boy who could grow into a man, a real man, who could take the place of the man who had died, accept the inheritance Kunstler carried? And still Kunstler had provided for this usurper, this changeling. No father, he felt, could claim the gratitude of his child more than he could.

And hers, too, the boy's mother: Hadn't he carried her through the doorway of their apartment? Hadn't he eaten with familial solemnity the meals she made and acquiesced to her urgent domesticity, to the electric percolator and the ridiculous knick-knacks, the saucered cups, flowered covers for the pillows, the matching twin beds on layaway? And hadn't she for her part accepted the bargain when she accepted his clothed body beside her naked one, the probing hands when to spoon was all she wanted and preferred, saying quietly in the morning as a gesture of her submission, as a vow that sealed their union, even though her eyes might be averted, "I enjoyed last night," in exchange for all of which he had given her a child?

Through the window Kunstler saw that the sun was rising. The morning's narrow cool would soon boil away. A pair of ripe, heavy summer flies buzzed stupidly against the screen. He put the paper back in his pocket and started the long job of doing up his shirt buttons.

·

With the claw of his right hand, Kunstler shifted down; the truck slowed. He watched the sidewalk rather than the street. At the corner they passed a building nearly hollow, with soft fire-black stripes above the windows. Jimmy looked up from the book he had been reading. "Oh wow, would you look at this place," Jimmy said. He pulled his sneaker off the dashboard and sat up. "I don't think I've been over here since the riots, man. That's some heavy shit."

Outside an empty-faced storefront sat a group of older men, all of them black, on lame and rusted office chairs pimpled with silver tape. Some younger men in tight shirts with heads like black cotton balls leaned on the vast hood of a vinyl-top sedan. Most necks seemed to turn slightly as the truck shuddered by, but otherwise nobody moved. A woman leaned in a doorway, her eyes closed. The truck's open windows filled with a smell of summer garbage, gasoline, the carbonized innards of the ruined building. A large pothole caught the right front wheel and everything in the cab lurched and bucked.

"Jesus, this can't be right." Jimmy pulled his binder from between the seats and started flipping through the pages.

"I don't know." Kunstler didn't look at him, or at the men who stood and sat around in the heat, at the woman in her doorway; he stared, he even spoke, as if he were completely alone, hardly bothering to be heard above the engine and the sounds of the city around them.

"You mean you don't know if we have a delivery over here?"

"What's that?"

"Abe, man, what's your bag? Do we have a delivery over here or what?"

"Don't we?"

"Wow, Jesus, Abe. Give me the route sheet. Come on, man, the route, huh? The route?" Still looking past Jimmy to the street rocking slowly along, Kunstler pulled a clipboard from the door pocket. Jimmy grabbed it from him. "Abe, man, what the hell? We don't have anything around here for a million miles."

"Sorry," Kunstler said without any change to his distant expression or tone. "I got turned around."

"Turned around?"

"There used to be a record store over here."

"Are you kidding me? I mean, there used to be a lot of goddamn shit, but we have work to do. What the hell?" The young man's expression was full of confused and annoyed inquiry, and for a moment Kunstler filled with the dream of blotting it from his face, replacing it with the blank look of pain. Instead Kunstler nodded as if accepting Jimmy's condolences. He said, "I haven't been sleeping, couple of nights. Maybe it's the heat; it hurts my hand. So I guess I got turned around. It's not like you were helping, is it? With your feet up and your face in your book there, like this was your living room. So just tell me where's next." Jimmy looked at him again, but Kunstler didn't look back. He didn't seem angry, or sorry, or even concerned at being lost. He just stared as if at a thing a million miles away, something he was trying to remember the shape of.

"From here? From here, man, it's like . . . Well, hell, I don't know. Give me a minute. A record store, Jesus. You want music, man, turn on the radio. We're going to be late for every goddamn thing now. The guys upstairs are going to shit all over us if we don't get everything off the truck by closing."

"Yeah," said Kunstler as he examined the passing buildings. What else had there been in the boy's room? He tried to think. The single bed, unmade, and across the short wedge of flaking linoleum floor a collage of things so disordered he had found it hard to focus on any one of them. What were they? He had seen schoolbooks, math and history. There were records, and the portable record player responsible by itself for the endless din now that Inez had finally stopped playing the radio all the goddamned time. There were some magazines with a crowd of costumed hippies on the covers. A few photos of the boy and his friends pinned to the wall by the bed. Some half-burned candles, the boy's dirty clothes piled on the chair: nothing.

When the truck reached the end of the block, he put it in neutral; the long stick fretted at his open palm, passing across the nubs of his missing fingers. There was no other traffic on the street, and they sat there silently for a minute. Sweat ran down Kunstler's temples, and his shirt where it touched the vinyl seat was soaked through, but he made no move to cool or dry himself. Instead he just sat and looked at nothing, his lips moving a little bit from time to time.

"I see it now," Jimmy said. He pulled a bandana from his jeans and wiped his face. "We better hang right."

"Okay."

"So? Abe? Turn right."

"Sure," Kunstler said. He pulled a cigarette from his shirt pocket, and lit it with a plastic lighter. He thought about the photos on the boy's wall. He thought briefly about pushing Jimmy out of the cab and driving straight to the apartment to look at them, kicking him with the full force of his heel to the chest or head, leaving him in the street to run uselessly after the truck. He thought, too, about the little bottle of gin he kept in the door pocket, a flask-shaped lump of plastic, how much it would help him to think if he could only drink some. Kunstler flexed the fingers of his claw and looked over at Jimmy.

"Christ, Abe. Do you want me to drive?"

Kunstler shook his head. "You grind the gears." He put the truck back in first and pulled hand over hand at the wheel.

At the first delivery Jimmy went inside to get a signature and have them open the storeroom door. To speed things up Kunstler unloaded the boxes off the gate and stacked them on the hand truck. Maybe, he thought, he should start instead with the child's mother: he would go to her, tell her the boy was dead. He would bring her a drink to comfort her, vermouth with a little gin, nothing too strong to start, enough just to dull the pain. It would smooth the path forward to the place where in her grief she could again be linked to him by need as she had been at the dance hall, stand alone with him in the spinning room of her drunkenness. During her pregnancy there had been the nausea she claimed to feel at the very smell of alcohol, but that was a long time ago. It was Kunstler who felt nauseous now. It was hot out, really hot, the sun was an open white sore in the sky oozing heat, the boxes were heavy, too heavy for one person, really. It felt like hours since his last drink.

But lying to the mother would mean that the boy had to be kept away, and that put Kunstler back where he had started, where he already was: looking for the boy, wandering around the city with Jimmy hanging over his shoulder, having to look God knows where. And then what? Pay him off, somehow, or if he didn't want to go, chase him away. Kunstler wondered desperately how long the boy had been planning on making his nasty little claims. Was it hours or years? Of course it didn't matter as long as he had kept them to himself. *Of course he has,* Kunstler thought. Anyone would know it was lies, after all. It was an unbelievable story to tell about someone who's a father, a factory worker, a married man, a soldier who had been wounded in the war. No one could believe it.

No, Kunstler decided, the boy was a coward, still digging in the dirt for the courage to say something. Is that what the miserable little monster used to mumble about in his sleep, the inarticulate sounds that had made Kunstler so nervous, the mindless puckering? He had been right all along: from the moment of its birth, Kunstler had known without question that the child was a grotesque inversion of everything he had worked for: not a strong or vital boy but a purple-fleshed weakling, his lip split and curling like a leaf. This was not his son.

Inez somehow didn't see the deception of the thing, insisting that they pour their money down the drain trying to make the boy look normal, when everyone knew that if it had been a dog born so deformed they would have drowned it. Worse was that the arrival of the boy had left Kunstler no way to start again, because it took all the girl's attention, all her affection—because she loved it. The girl who had over-looked so much could easily see Kunstler's disappointment. He hadn't found room left in himself to hide it, not with all the rest, not after all the other defeats, the setbacks and disillusionments, after losing the factory and with it the money to keep the car, the apartment in the old neighborhood. He thought of his lost fingers, the relics of his old life now disintegrated to the bone.

He had expected that once the baby was out of her, Inez would be herself again, that they would get back to their routines, their places, their drinks and dances. He had looked forward to diving again into nights of boozy contact, where her naked body was his, but instead it had disappeared from him. He would gladly have continued trying with her, doing whatever it took to have a real son, the true son that was Kunstler's goal and right, his offering to the spirit of the dead man who was his own true father, reassembled in himself.

On Sunday afternoons before the boy had been born Kunstler and his girl would sometimes put on nice clothes to walk arm in arm through Trenton, a man and a woman strolling with the others in the sunshine and stopping sometimes to sit on a bench, where she would rest her head on his shoulder and he would read the paper. No one passing could have found fault in Kunstler and his girl. He had never been unfaithful to her.

When the boxes were done he climbed back into the cab and took a drink from the plastic bottle. Right away he felt better: less hot, less confused. A solution was possible, even if it wasn't clear yet exactly how to achieve it. Jimmy was waving at him in the side mirror. Kunstler turned away and drank again, a long, mind-clearing stream of gin, then slipped the bottle in the door pocket, climbed down again, and walked back to the lowered gate.

Jimmy was complaining. "You couldn't have put the hand truck on the curb first, Abe? Now we have to heave this whole pile of stuff up the side."

Kunstler said, "I guess we can do it without either of us dying," but the curb was high and it was harder than he had expected. He had to lift from the street side, and as the truck finally jerked clear to the sidewalk, he jumped with a short cry of pain.

"What happened?"

"Shit," said Kunstler. "My thumb got caught in the frame." It was his bad hand. The crease around the nail was filling with blood and the skin was already changing color.

"Shit," agreed Jimmy. "All right, let's do this and while we're in there we can see if they have any ice or something."

Jimmy took the hand truck and Abe followed him down a brick and concrete alley to a metal delivery door covered in graffiti. Inside waited a couple of black men in coveralls with no shirts underneath. "Come on through," one of them said, waving a gloved hand as if he were guiding a steamroller or a locomotive. The space was crowded, and to follow the customers inside meant navigating a dark goat path between ceiling-high columns of boxes. Several times Abe had to lean down to help Jimmy shift the truck sideways. He steadied himself on one of the columns.

"Careful," Jimmy said to him. "Don't, you know."

"Don't what?"

Jimmy whispered. "Don't get blood on everything." Abe saw it already covered his palm. He wiped his hand on his pants.

The hand truck got jammed again, and this time caught Abe's foot when they shifted it. He started swearing. "What the hell do these people need all this fucking garbage for anyway?" he said.

Jimmy looked over at the customers. "Ignore him," he said. "He's thinks he's joking, but his sense of humor hasn't been the same since D-day. Shell shock, you know?"

Back out in the alley, Jimmy said, "You have blood all over your shirt."

Kunstler looked down at it and shrugged. He said, "It had to go somewhere if it wasn't supposed to end up on their precious floor. You didn't ask."

"Ask?"

"About the ice."

"Yeah. I didn't think they would be very interested in helping you. In case you're wondering, it's because you came off like an asshole. Maybe there's a deli on the way where we can stop and get you something." Jimmy pulled his bandana out and handed it to Abe. "Then we can be extra late, and I can get home just in time to leave for work tomorrow."

"Fuck you," said Abe, but he accepted the bandana and wrapped it around his thumb.

"Sure," said Jimmy. "I know, man. Same to you," but Kunstler was already heading quickly back to the truck. He had things to do. He had to manufacture a solution, and to do that he had to find the boy. Too much was at stake. All this other stuff was just a waste of time. *Let the pain be a reminder,* he thought.

--- * ---

"I just get nervous, I guess," Art told Bets as they put sheets on the small folding bed in the stifling, dirty little back room. The sheets were old and clean, but wilted from the heat. The summer had turned everything soft: the tar in the streets, the buzzing of the thick, fat flies, people's clothes, the stems of the flowers in the park, the viscous air. The world lay flat, everything was exhausted, beaten down by the humidity. Art noticed—because of course despite himself he was looking— that in the heat even Bets' nipples were too lazy to get up from their soft beds under her tank top. The little room was especially hot, despite having been exposed like the others when Dion had gone on his mysterious, violent frenzy against the apartment's doors, practically tearing them from the frames. "I think maybe I don't like the idea of people seeing me when I'm asleep, when I'm not in control of myself, you know?" Art said, and rocking on her bare feet so her flowered skirt waved like a meadow Bets asked him, sweetly and joyously teasing and yet somehow also with real curiosity, "I guess what I want to know is, who's in control of you asleep, if not you?" and to cover her smile let fall the parted curtain of dirty hair.

Bets would joke sometimes that he had followed her home from the park like a lost puppy, and in moments like this Art knew she wasn't far wrong: he couldn't tell her that at home an open door had forever been a fearful thing, a crack through which an ocean might have poured in to drown him. He was as ashamed as a whipped dog at how fully he accepted his family's world, ashamed of the fact that something as small as turning a doorknob when his father was home scared him with a fear so lasting and deep that the unthinking part of him recoiled from Dion's wounded wall, saw in the empty space a deviation from the natural order, a dangerous sacrilege.

He had learned the danger even before Uncle Jacks had been revealed in the open door to the landing, standing there in his factory blues as uncertainly as a stranger, breathing winter steam through his open mouth and looking down at Art—who was just a little kid then, maybe not even in school yet. He let him yell, "It's Uncle Jacks!" before demanding and accepting Art's tiny hand in his huge, cold fingers and walking down the narrow hallway with him, the child and the enormous man each somehow leading the other, Art in his socks taking the biggest sliding steps he could to where his mother waited for them in the kitchen. Her color drained as Jacks told her in his great, dull voice that something had happened, that there had been an accident, saying, "That's the thing," again and again like a prayer: "That's the thing, and I came to tell you," all the time holding Art's hand in his own the way someone might carry a slip of crumbling paper he didn't dare lose. He didn't let go even when Art's mother nodded, and started to cry, asking in a new voice, one that slipped somewhere deeper than was hers, "What kind of accident?" The way her face melted wet and red filled Art with terror, and he wanted to leave, to run and hide. He tried to pull away, but Jacks seemed not to notice, just held him, an immensity that exerted no real pressure but was still inescapable.

"He didn't say a word to no one," Jacks said. "That's the thing, he just walked out, I guess. People heard a noise, but when they got to his machine, he wasn't there. They went looking for him, you know, all the guys, they followed the ... They tried to find him."

Art wasn't sure now how many days it had been before his father had shown up, finally, in the same way: he, too, standing in the open door as if for the first time, unfocused eyes that had never willingly rested on the boy but now worse. His gaze swam even past Art's mother, who herself was so tired from her panicked waiting that she had almost ignored his pathetic knocking, whispering that she had thought it might be something else, mistaken it for an engine, maybe, backfiring and failing somewhere in the distance.

Art's father was unsteady, dressed in another man's over-sized clothes, right arm wrapped in a huge club of off-white bandage from which his remaining fingers protruded like slug's eyes, what they later found to be a child's torn sweater tied around his neck as a scarf. He swayed for a moment as if about to tumble before at last shuffling through, Inez and Art trailing behind to the bedroom, where Abe pulled the curtains and lay on his bed in the dark and said with a downy voice almost as foreign as the coat he lay down in, "Don't touch me. Don't you dare touch me," then slept whimpering through a store of tablets he had carried home loose in the pocket of some other man's pants. When one pill wore off, Art's father would come awake with a start and a wordless, grinding noise of pain and reach into the pocket for another and chew it, clenching his eyes shut and rocking his cradled arm until at last he was dragged back into his furious medical slumber.

Art sometimes listened furtively from just outside his parents' room, crouching at the threshold as if answering a dare and worrying the ridge of his harelip with an uneasy tongue, but the violence of his father's movements, the tearing depth of his groans, would always scare him away. Even sitting with his mother in the kitchen or lying in the dark dust of safety under his bed, Art could hear his father agonizing, sometimes barking *Don't touch me* through the tranquilized fear and pain at the shadowy emptiness, at the groping onlookers who didn't exist, and then, when the pills had run out and he switched to booze, yelling for whiskey, which he drank in huge, overflowing gulps straight from the mouth of the bottle, his throat working like a piston, the liquid overflowing down his face and into his clothes. Each time Inez asked questions or mentioned doctors he responded with vicious threats.

Finally Jacks was summoned. He had of course been waiting faithfully and came at an eager trot, at last allowed to bring Abe's suit and other belongings in the cardboard box to which they had been moved from a locker at the factory. Kunstler remained so long in the bathroom getting dressed that Jacks had to take Art down the stairs and behind the building to pee, the boy hiding in the tall weeds that grew around the rusted and buckled basement hatch, his urine steaming in the cold winter air. As they stood there in the garbage-strewn yard the big man had started talking with a burst, as if he had been waiting for someone to ask and understood finally that no one would, and so told the only person he could trust not to judge him for his gentle, aggravating simplicity. He talked down to Art's back about the fingers that had been on the floor by Abe Kunstler's machine, two wads of dead flesh in a pool of blood like goldfish spilled from their bowl. Immediately the trickle of urine had ceased and Art had stood frozen, still holding himself, trapped in his wide-legged stance, until Uncle Jacks had asked if he needed help with his fly and Art had numbly accepted. His father would never return to the factory, and his fingers, which Jacks had carefully and secretly buried in an old stuffing box, never left it. They were not mentioned any more than Art's harelip, his mother's quiet, compacted misery, his father's hidden wound, and the other things—a list abstruse, hazy, variable—that only Art's father could speak of, so that no answer could be made when he would grab Art's face and complain in a blast of whiskey breath that despite all the money wasted on doctors, the child still had a mouth like a fish, or when he boasted of his suffering in the war. A leaden silence was closed on these things like a box lid, barred with fear and reprehension and his father's endless anger. Even poor, huge Uncle Jacks feared it. "Don't tell your old man," he said to Art as they made their way over the broken concrete back around to the front door. "Don't tell him about I buried them, I mean, the fingers. I think maybe he wouldn't like it."

Art reproduced the family rituals with all the perfect adaptability of a child. He did it naturally, efficiently, and without question, unthinkingly finding and closing doors of his own, hiding from his raging father in the hall closet's shallow floating forest of coat belts with the funk of mothballs and shoes, or in the space at the bottom of the narrow kitchen cupboard, learning to pull it shut by the bent metal catch, careful to snatch his fingers away before the housing snapped to. In his bedroom he made a kind of door by hiding behind the sheets and blankets hanging from his bed. He would crawl along the cold floor with his toys for company and think of his father's fingers in their dark lake of blood, and of the even, brown tarnish Uncle Jacks said it left behind on the concrete factory floor, a trail leading the aghast die men and managers through the building's front doors before it sank tracelessly into the black depths of the asphalt outside.

So when Bets finally left the hot little room through the fearsome doorless gap in the wall, Art turned out the lamp and settled cautiously and guiltily under the just-made bed, wrestling out of his jeans only once he felt hidden. When he was high, he had the impression he was conscious of every-thing, a sensation that was both beautiful and alarming, like carrying the world in the back of your eyeballs, felt but invis-ible. Lying there he had a sense of the belly of the room as if seeing it from outside, cut open to expose the strange cluster of its entrails: the unpainted plasterwork on the walls, the one chair, the spare metal bed, and himself.

There was enough light from the hallway that after his eyes adjusted he could just make out above him the lattice of twisted wires and behind them the mattress, the straight lines of the ticking, the dark cloud-shaped stains. Below him the floorboards ran unevenly through the dust that shifted with the air and the heat of the room and floated in and out of his nostrils.

As he drifted towards sleep he thought about the body seen from under a bed in his parents' room, the hard and ungener-ous body of his father's lover, his mother's rival. He couldn't remember any more why he had gone someplace where he knew from terrible experience he wasn't supposed to be, only that he had thought he was alone in the apartment until he heard his father: the coughing and heavy drink-slow walk approaching from the living room, moving like a slow storm up the short hall. Art had curled in hiding at the farthest end of the bed's protective canopy, and when the sounds entered the bedroom and were followed by the locking of the door he covered his face with his hands, as if they were a door that could shield him from discovery. Uncertain noises and whispered muttering reached him like a distant siren through the fear that throbbed and crackled in his ears. When he dared at last to peek he saw it, visible only an instant as it passed the barely parted curtain of hanging sheets and blankets: a pair of legs and hips and breasts scant where his mother was full and soft, the first naked body of his experience and therefore impressive, arousing, even as he feared and despised it. This was the sign of his father's treachery, and it could not be unseen, though Art immediately covered his eyes again and tried to wish himself away, cowered through the passing of an unknowable time until he at last recognized the unlocking of the bedroom door. Even then his eyes stayed closed for the eternity that followed until he thought he heard his father's shoes and the slamming of the front door. It was a while before his racing heart slowed enough to let him hear if silence was what followed.

Already as he scuttled nervously down the hallway to his own room, it was there, inescapable: an image he never wanted but carried with him, just as he carried with him the twist of his harelip and the sound of his own voice, one that would appear uninvited in his dreams, intruding amidst the faces and imagined bodies of the others that he desired, floating in reverberation through his fantasy of Dion and Bets. It crept into the memory of the time he had spied them through the doorless gap in their bedroom wall, Bets on top of Dion, her breasts caught in a thin blade of morning sunlight. That night beneath the cot his dream was stained even darker by the knowledge that Dion had his lottery number, and suddenly the three slipping bodies were joined in Art's half-sleeping mind by the television's terrifying, bloody images of the war.

.

Dion had become different. It was the lottery that changed him. It wasn't surprising and still Art was surprised. He had somewhere within believed Dion to be as imperturbable, as absolute and as distant as the weather. He had always appeared unflinching in exactly the situations that Art found the most agonizing, even almost unbearable.

Now that ease was gone. The change had come slowly—so slowly that it would be hard to pick the moment it began, to say if it was days or even weeks before the lottery that he started to show signs of worry, as if he were receiving warnings from the future and decoding them hour by hour. Not even Bets had understood yet that it was the draft on Dion's mind the hot, oppressive evening that he had torn down the doors, working viciously, blindly, without explanation, leaving his bare arms and chest covered in scratches and cuts, small red accents in the olive skin. Bets protested only briefly over the door to the bathroom, but it came out anyway. While Dion raged through the apartment, Art and Bets lay on the floor of the kitchen, just the two of them, passing a joint and looking up at the pattern of light the streetlamps scattered through Bets' jungle of ferns. Art said it reminded him of a time once when he had crawled into his parents' bedroom at night and been misled by a confusing tangle of streetlight so faint it was depthless but still seemed to recede like the opening to a tunnel. The pattern was reflected from a tall mirror on the wall, so that the room turned in around itself, and he had become unsure of which way he was heading. Suddenly he was scared, and his actions grew hurried, and finally he tripped over something in the dark. His father had been furious at being woken up.

Bets said something, but Art didn't hear; he had caught a glimpse in the pot smoke and that filigreed light of the stranger, the hard-breasted woman, the body that ran through his dreams. He heard again the sound, his father's footsteps and wheezing breath, that had driven him under the empty bed in his parents' room in the dark in case the old man found him searching the apartment for the comfort of his mother. Art wasn't supposed to go in there, had been punished for it again and again, but still he had wanted her and so walked very quietly through the hallway blackness, careful not to stub his toes, with both hands held up to the passing wall in guidance until his fingers met the frame of his parents' bedroom door. His own breath whistled in his ears like a wind, and on all fours now, he pushed the door to enter. The hinge softly complained. His head filled with a rush of blood and fear and he waited, heart convulsing so wildly it felt as if he might bounce. He didn't dare move at all until the churning blood retreated.

He had to wait before asking Bets to repeat herself. "I said, I think it's beautiful," she told him. "The way the light comes through." Art took a long hit and explored the tips of his harelip with his tongue before exhaling. When he was younger he had hated that mirror in his parents' room: it was the only one in the apartment low enough to show him what he least wanted to see, the rent, cockeyed nose above the tight swirl of his mouth. It was only in the dark that it offered him deception.

"Yes," he said finally. "I think so, too."

"Are you going back to school in the fall?" Bets asked suddenly.

He thought for a minute before admitting, "Man, I don't know."

"I wish you would, Art. I mean it, really."

"Dion calls high school indoctrination."

"He also says strategy is everything. What if the war isn't over before you graduate? You have a better chance of deferment if you're in college. Especially since you're the only son, you could say you need the education to support your family." At the word *family* he made a noise. She rolled over to hug him then and into his ear said, "Baby, I'm already so worried about Dion. Don't make me worry about you, too. Not yet." Art moved away so she wouldn't notice his erection.

After the lottery Dion and Bets argued, the first time Art had ever heard them like that, Bets yelling that she would drive him, that minute, to Canada, and Dion refusing, noises so unlike the usual sounds they made when alone of whispering and sex and sometimes Bets laughing with a husky sound like someone shuffling across a field of dry leaves. When the fight was over, Dion didn't say anything about it, just took Art by the arm and dragged him up the fire escape to the roof under the folding light of the setting sun, where Art watched impotently as Dion then paced around, smoking his way through a pack of cigarettes and a dime bag's worth of grass. It was as if his whole nature had been distorted by the restlessness of his thoughts, which raced to explore all the possible outcomes, prisons and battlefields, pain and horror, confinement and repression. It scared Art so much he retreated back down the shuddering ladder to the kitchen as soon as he could, leaving Dion to shout at the nighttime.

"You know he can't go," Bets told him. She was at the table staring down at an untouched cup of tea, her face puffed from crying. "Dion can't be drafted. They'll destroy him. The person we know will be gone." She looked at Art and he nodded. "And he can't go to jail for dodging. That's nearly as bad. Either way, if they get their hands on him, they'll make it a goal to rearrange his brain. I mean, Jesus, listen to him. They're hurting him already and they haven't even got him yet."

In the dark kitchen Bets told Art something she said she'd never told anyone else except Dion: about how her father had killed himself with a Chinese-made pistol he had taken from the still-shuddering corpse of a uniformed boy in a patch of woodland in Korea. There had been a raiding party that caught her father's patrol off guard with a mortar and sent them scattering into the trees. Concussed and half deafened by the explosion, her father had stumbled into the boy, a Chinese soldier, and they fought, rolling in the leaves and dirt. In the end her father stabbed him in the throat with a stick. His own Colt lost somewhere, his ears ringing, he had carried the boy's weapon in front of him, his arm held straight, elbow locked, and pointed it at every imagined sound in turn and once or twice fired it into the trees as he staggered his way back to his battalion, scattering groups of men when he swung wildly through the tattered camp with the pistol held in front of him as if the tiny hole of the barrel were all that allowed him to see. He refused to let go of it even when two men he didn't know—a radio operator and an artillery mechanic—had finally grabbed him from behind and pressed him into the mud. It was not long before that or after it— or maybe it was even just exactly while he had been driving a piece of wood through the throat of the Chinese boy in the trees, he didn't know—that his daughter had been born, although it would be several days before he learned about it. The information had to follow him north from Seoul and then back again to the hospital where he was sent for evaluation. All this he had written to her in the letter he left behind.

"It was somewhere they called Triangle Hill. It's in North Korea now," she said. "Thousands of people died fighting over this place, and because it was a failure, no one in America has ever heard of it. You've never heard of it, right? I don't even know what the real name is of the place."

Art wondered impotently what to say, desperate to speak although he knew that nothing spoken would make a difference. Even before they met, Art had wished he could be like Dion, like any of the imagined Dions conjured in his lonely childhood, distantly observed across classrooms and playgrounds or on television screens, who in his dream he would occupy like a possessing spirit: fluent, assured, cool. Instead he was like poor Jacks, so confounded by words and yet desperate to use them.

Art couldn't answer Dion, either, when later he and Bets lay stoned on the roof and Dion called to them from his aimless, recurring, grassed-up procession, talking with all the strange fluency that came from a skull full of smoke. He yelled about the majesty of the darkness, about the impossibility of anything existing without its opposite. They looked south to where the huge sign on the bridge glowed behind the low skyline, lit the clouds red, and though Art couldn't see the words he knew them like a prayer: THE WORLD TAKES.

Now it seemed the world would take Dion. For one beautiful and terrifying moment, Art saw Dion and the orgiastic god as one, a powerful being touched with death, robbed of immortality by human transgressions. He felt as if he were at the very top of a tree looking down on the city blinking in the dark, out over a huge horizon of expanding darkness, and that Dion by his simple will had bent it to a ground he hadn't known was there. Then reality rushed in again, and Art cupped his face in his hands as if to trap within himself the rising desire he felt to speak, and he thought again of Jacks trying so desperately on the day of the accident to build some comfort out of a material he would never master, telling Art's mother, who wasn't even listening, "They wanted that someone should tell you, and I said I would do it, and I made Butler drive me here, and he was happy to. Well not, not happy. Not happy, you know," before finally collapsing with miserable relief into speechlessness, a willed look of vacancy on his face. Art guessed that he looked the same as Dion stared at him through the unhappy humid nighttime: ashamed at the comfort of his own silence, horrified by his own impotence. He was limited, he was insignificant, tiny, and worst of all he was thankful when Dion turned at last again furiously to admire and admonish the sky.

·

The next morning Dion was out. They hadn't heard him leave, but they found him in the park as surely as if they had bloodhounded him through the sun-greased streets by his smell, which Art knew was fennel and sweat and unwashed denim. The park is where Turtle was. Dion and a group of people Art didn't know that well were passing joints around a circle with Turtle, who crouched on his heels, hugely bearded and impenetrably grimy, still in the fatigues and boots he had been wearing when they handed him his discharge in Da Nang. There were rumors he had sworn not to take them off until every American was out of Vietnam, and that some or most or all of the dirt was really blood.

Turtle had been living in the park nearly six months by then, and during that whole time Art had not known him to stop talking about the draft and the war except sometimes to sleep or shit or evade the cops for an hour or two. He certainly didn't stop now to eat: instead he talked through every bite, as if there wasn't space enough inside him for food and the story of his war to live together and the one had to make way for the other. Art desperately wanted to eat.

While Turtle talked and chewed, the girls watched Dion, the knotty vines of his arms, his wine-stain lips, the brown fox eyes quarried in the high-cheeked stone of his face, with looks that said they hadn't noticed yet that the habitual ease of his body had been broken across the restlessness of his mind, left him straining like an animal against the slow, inflexible strap of time.

"All along the process there's hope, you know," Turtle was saying. "And they dangle this hope in front of you, and the alternatives, well. Man, they don't seem like alternatives at all from the way they tell it. Like they say, 'You can go to basic training, or you can go to jail, it's up to you. Ever been to jail? Ever try to have a life with a criminal record?' And they're still dangling that little bit of hope, you know. You might wash out, or you might get sent to Japan or Germany or Korea. So you get on the bus and you hope for the best. Then you find out, congratulations! They're sending you to Vietnam."

Turtle patted at his various pockets and produced a packet of ketchup, which he tore open with his teeth and squeezed out onto some slices of white bread he pulled from a brown paper bag. He looked around at everyone through his dirty, chewing face before he started again. "So, now the options are get on the plane or go to military jail, which makes real jail sound like fun."

The short, balled-up trees surrounding the small square of grass where they sat shrugged off a breeze. Turtle always made sure he was someplace where he could keep one eye looking through the metal fence that gave out onto the street, in case the cops came, and he took a second to stare as if at something a hundred miles away. Art looked back over his shoulder but saw nothing.

"So," said Turtle, still staring out across the dying grass, "you get on the fucking plane, and you shit bricks, but you're still hoping for the best. By the time you're on the front and people are shooting at you, they don't even bother threatening you with jail or court martial any more. They don't need to— man, there's bullets! Your choices are act like a soldier or get killed, so you just do what your body tells you: you start shooting and running and hope you don't get killed. For a while you hope that you don't get some other guy killed, either, until the terrible day you realize that really, honestly, if you tell yourself the fucking truth for just one goddamn time in your life, if it has to be somebody, you would rather it be anybody other than you. And, man, that's the very worst part of it."

He stopped and shifted his weight from one squatting thigh to the other. For a moment he scratched at his beard with his knuckles, and Art thought maybe he had finished, but he started again, saying, "They're always talking about how the army and war will make a man out of you, but I was never a man there, if by man you mean human. I would have ripped any one of you people apart to save my own life, and that's the truth. It might sound crazy, but sitting there wishing some other bastard would get it in my place, I made a promise to God. I promised that if I got back alive, I would tell everyone I met about what a pointless, useless hell it is we're building over there. And I would say, 'Whatever you do, whatever the big boys say or threaten you with, don't go.' And if you have to break the law, you break it. That's just self-defense, right? The law's trying to kill you, literally kill you, by sending you off to die." Suddenly he seemed completely exhausted. He face closed in on itself, his mouth half open on the cud of bread he had stopped chewing.

"Governor Reagan said we could cover North Vietnam with parking lots and have everybody back by Christmas," one of the girls said.

Turtle didn't look up at first. He was drawing something in the dirt with his finger. "When the hell did he say that?" he asked finally in a quieter voice than before.

"Nineteen sixty-five."

"Shit. Well, I guess he was off by a day or two. I wish I had it in me to laugh about it, but I know guys who are probably dying right now to make that cocksucker's bullshit dream come true."

It was clear Dion wasn't listening. Art watched him across the circle of kids. Art loved Dion's olive skin and curly hair, the strange power of his androgyny, the strength and vulner-ability, empathy and severity, the narrowness of his hips and the fullness of his mouth. Concern worked across Dion's beau-tiful face like a storm, and Art followed its unhappy prog-ress. Later Dion talked to Turtle alone, the two wandering away, and Art knew, as everyone must have, that they were talking about how to dodge, because eventually dodging was what every eighteen-year-old with a draft card came to talk to Turtle about. It was a consultation with the oracle of the antiwar, the only man in Trenton anyone knew to ask. Even in the park the air was thick with paranoia and fear, with stories of kids getting busted by the guys they thought were helping them defer, and about how entrapment wasn't an issue when it came to the draft, because if they didn't jail you on dodging, they got you for the army. What the hell was the difference, Dion had once said, except that the army was probably worse?

"What's up with Dion?" one of the kids asked.

"Wednesday night," a skinny girl said. "The lottery. They really nailed him."

"Oh, shit. How low?" They all looked at Bets, but she didn't say anything.

"Pretty low, I think," said the skinny one, rocking nervously as she spoke. She looked again at Bets. "Six. I think that's what he told Turtle before. And no back door. I mean, no dependents, right? And let's face it, he's not going to be going to college or anything, and the new rules, man. I mean, even if some pregnant chick would say it was Dion knocked her up, it wouldn't mean a thing, so he's the one, you know. The real one-A."

"I don't get it," said a greasy-looking boy. "Why doesn't the guy just take a drive to Canada, you know? Lots of people are going." That's when Bets got up suddenly with her big fringed leather bag and left, and Art followed. The girl was still talking as they left about how the war was a genocide perpetrated against the black people of America. "Middle-class white kids are welcome wherever," she was saying. "It's not so easy to find a new country when you're black."

Bets and Art waited together for Dion on the park's north side, where the city glimmered in the gathering heat. Everything around them was temperature and light: the sun rolled down the walls and windows of the buildings, flashed off the sudden windshields of the cars and buses, lay molten on the sidewalk. Bets dug in her bag for her weed and they smoked while walking in little circles. Art listened to his empty stom-ach grumble and moan, the pot making him even hungrier. Dion arrived finally. He climbed the fence and as if speaking to himself explained, "What Turtle says is, the only sure thing is to fail the physical way before you get anywhere near the induction center, because you can't beat the system using the system's rules." The plan itself revolved around a first-year hospital resident known as Dr. Dodge. He knew what he was doing, Dion said, had done it before.

Still, though, Dion didn't seem comfortable with it, some-how. He talked around something that he didn't seem to want to admit, and he talked for some time before it dawned on Art what it was all coming to, slowly and unwillingly: that Dion, who lived by sharing and taking what was unwanted and refusing to desire what couldn't be his, had a plan in mind, but no idea how he would afford it. It was in the voice of a man admitting sin that Dion finally said, "I'm going to need money, man."

Art had never even heard him call it money before, but always something else, something that reduced it, belittled it somehow: moolah, clams, dough, "the long green." *We got to get us some of that dirty bread, man.*

Art was dizzied, disoriented by pot and hunger but even more, he felt, by admiration for Dion, and in a kind of dream made from Dion's talk he thought of something one of his teachers had told him, a story about the way people had pro-tected statues from being bombed in Europe during the war, and the teacher, one of those men who stood alone at the front of the classroom as if it were empty and talked as if to himself about a thing he had only just glimpsed, said that they had done it not because a statue had ever fed a man, and not even because anyone had ever even stopped to look at a statue that they could remember, let alone been touched by it or inspired or noticed its beauty. It was just so they could know they had acted, know they had protected something, anything, from the overwhelming situation, taken some tiny stand against the irresistible tide of history. "Do you understand?" the teacher had asked the silent room. It was only now that Art suddenly did: that the attempt was its own monument, and that he, too, could build one, now, by a simple act of the will. It would be, Art felt with a kind of thrill, magnificent in just that same way to keep something as beautiful as Dion alive through the darkness of the era, and so before he had even thought it through, he found himself telling them, "I might have some money."

The others stopped and looked at him with faces that almost made Art laugh. He said, "Well, hey, man, not me. But I might know where to get some. Like for an emergency. And this is, well . . . Jesus, you know."

Dion seemed to rise on the news, so it was only to Bets that Art admitted it was hardly certain: his father had long suspected his mother of hoarding cash. Art was like the others, he had nothing. "The thing is, honestly," Art admitted, "I stole forty cents from your purse so I could buy a coffee at the diner and use a bathroom with a door." Still, he felt sure it was there somewhere, because if there was one thing his father knew it was how much everyone was making and spending, how much should be left then for booze. On the day of their big fight Art had found the old man slowly tearing the place apart in search of what he had always felt by rights was his. Art was sure, too, that if he asked her, if he explained the urgency, if he made what he had just sensed clear somehow, his mother would give him what they needed, or at least what she could. It might be enough, and if not it might come so near to it that the rest was something they could hustle from somewhere, friends and strangers. All they had to do, he told himself, was avoid his father.

That meant he couldn't take them to the apartment to wait for his mother. He never knew when his father would be home. The old man was always calling in sick, by which he really meant drunk, and Art wasn't ready to confront him again, not yet. He wasn't sure he ever would be. He sensed somehow that Bets expected it of him, or at least expected him to desire it. He knew she was someone who would look forward with a kind of athlete's anticipation to the showdown, the bold and honest confrontation, but he had attempted it and found that the fear—of his father, of course, his unquenchable rage, but also of his own sudden and unfamiliar honesty—had been too much to handle, had overwhelmed him. The words as they rose had stolen all the air from his lungs and left him breathless, his legs had felt almost too weak to carry him when the moment came to run.

He told Bets only half the story: that he and his father had argued yet again over the draft, and Art's clothes, which to Art's father were somehow permanently linked. The two of them could barely be in the same room together without fighting. They disagreed about Nixon and segregation and the draft, a script they followed with the predictability of a streetlight coming on at dusk, Art's father talking about it all in terms of what he called a man's duty, of patriotism and fatherland, all the usual empty stuff. Art knew but somehow couldn't express why this was beside the point, that there was something deeper, more basic, something about the rules, the system, but the idea he was after remained so soft in his mind, so abstract and distant and intangible, that he couldn't with his constraining mouth find the words. Without ammunition of his own, Art would again find himself falling back on things he had heard others say, things he believed were true but that were not the thing he wanted or needed to express, as when he said, "So a bunch of villagers should burn to death in their fields because you think that makes a man out of some poor guy from Iowa? That proves we love our country?"

Abe had been kneeling as he ran mechanically through his list of grievances with a generation who mocked responsibility, who had no idea of sacrifice, a generation of boys who needed to become men. He was searching through the nameless third- or fourth-hand piece of furniture that sat behind the sofa in the living room, the one in which were stored all the unused things Art's mother nevertheless kept as safe as relics, the cheap department-store teacups, tiny wineglasses, little circles of lace gone yellow. "What the hell do you know about being a man, with your long hair and your sissy clothes? It's all a big joke to you. You've never had to take responsibility for anything. I have news for you: that's not how it works. Do you think I could have done what I did if I went around dressed like that, with long hair, and no collar, wearing a bunch of voodoo necklaces like a fruit? Work at a factory? Support a family?"

"Are you kidding? You haven't worked at the factory since I was a little kid. Mom pays for everything around here; we all know that. That's why you're crawling around on the floor, isn't it? Trying to find her money because you spent all of yours on liquor?"

Was that when his father had stood up? He didn't tell Bets the rest: the awful admission he'd made, the unprecedented effect it had on his father.

Art said to Bets, "My mother is probably at her job anyway." They walked, Art thought, the way things float in a puddle, sometimes pulled apart, sometimes pressed together, and he could never understand what the force was that made the difference.

"So we'll go by her job," said Bets.

"It's always changing. She's, you know." He stopped to inhale. "She's not like a normal cleaning lady, like always working at the same place. She works for a company that does a whole bunch of the big office buildings downtown, a couple of them maybe in the suburbs. You never know where they're going to send her. She could be anywhere."

"Well," said Dion. "Then we wait."

"No, we don't," said Bets. "We don't have long before either you go to the induction center or become a criminal. We can't wait. What's the name of the company? We can look it up. If they've got customers all around, they're going to be in the book."

"I don't really know. I mean, we never really talk about her work much. I just know that her boss is called Mr. Helms. My uncle Jacks might know where to find her, maybe. They work for the same people, I think, only . . ."

"Only what?" Bets asked in a voice that wasn't angry, or demanding, or even concerned, but instead just strangely empty, as if hollowed out and waiting for the anger or demand or concern that might need to come. Art thought about Jacks, huge in every way except his mind, his deafening voice, his ungainly lumbering, and above all his massive, overwhelming simplicity. "I don't see him very often. I mean, I'm not sure if he's working today, too. And honestly, you know, he's a little strange," he said finally.

Dion did his best to enjoy this silver lining. "Hey," he said without much conviction. "Sounds like my kind of guy."

"It can't hurt us to try," Bets said. "All right?"

"Yeah, all right," echoed Art. "So, I guess let's go."

.

Art had often enough stood behind his mother on the same steps in front of the same door to the same lodging house, listening to Mrs. Lakatos, shirt buttoned high on her neck and topped with a bow, offer in a resentful tone to call Douglas. It was Jacks who appeared when this other man had been named and sent for, something that had given Art a terrible, bitter feeling of betrayal that wouldn't be tamed, even when Jacks had said consolingly, jokingly, but also with a hint of pride, "That's right: I'm Mr. Douglas Jackson, Esquire. But you can still call me Jacks, because I'm Jacks to my friends and we're always going to be friends, right?" When his mother reminded him that his own name was something else, asking, "Are you Art, or are you Arthur? Or are you both?" the fear that he was being somehow mocked had only deepened his pout. Arthur was a stranger to him, a threat. It was a name belonging to someone lurking on the stairs outside the apartment door, waiting one day to take over his body.

Inside the stuccoed little building was the room where Art and his mother would spend the night when Art's father was too drunk, too angry, too violent. In the rented little room Art's mother and Jacks sat rigidly, aware all the time of Mrs. Lakatos sneaking across the landing, or standing halfway down the stairs, one ear apparently always open in anticipatory outrage. Art would play on the floor while the two adults made small talk and then eventually, inevitably, had their argument about who should take the bed. Art's mother always lost, of course, because gallantry towards women was an immovable pillar of Jacks' simple creed. Finally Art and his mother would sleep there, clothed, only their shoes removed and put carefully by the door so they wouldn't trip in the night if Art needed the bathroom, and Uncle Jacks would try his best to sleep on his two chairs pulled together the way men did in the movies, even though he was clearly too big and would always end up on the floor, on one occasion with a crash that woke them all.

For years this had been Art's neighborhood, but he never knew it that well beyond the grocery store and the Laundro-mat, the way to school, his family's home and the Lakatos house, which by a faded handmade sign still offered reason-able rates and steam heat. His mother hadn't liked him to play with the rough boys from down the block, who were all bigger and older, born the year the war ended. His father had never really liked for any of them, mother, father, or son, to leave the apartment if they didn't have to. He certainly didn't want Art to associate with the immigrant families, the ones he called Hungies: the beefy, red-faced Polish kids whose fat, low-set grandmothers waddled like kerchiefed penguins between swaying baskets of groceries, strong boys who picked on Art, bringing his mother down into the street to yell at them and their parents. "Every time you go out, you make trouble," his father once told him in a hot, gin-scented hiss. "I'd rather see you dead than let you ruin everything with your goddamn mess." It was the flat, polished stare as he said it that had made Art frightened. He crawled under his bed afterwards and stayed there all day.

Art looked back at Dion and Bets and then pressed the bell, a toy-like button set in the middle of the door that didn't really ring, but just went *click clack*. He pressed it twice. "Jacks isn't really my uncle, you know," he said as they waited. "He's my father's friend, back from when they both worked at this factory together."

"Hey, that's okay," Dion told him. "We're not worried about his family tree."

"I just mean—"

"I know what you mean. Don't flip your wig. It's all cool."

Pale Mrs. Lakatos answered, diminished of course, her clothes and face both threadbare, but her dry disapproval still ample, undulled it seemed by time and familiarity with the incorrigible world, her shirt still tied at the neck with a bow despite the weather. There was talcum powder caught in the wrinkled skin around the top of her collar, which was loose and limp, just as her half of the semidetached building was now loose around her: as she aged, she had grown scared of taking in new people. When the old ones moved away, or died, their rooms stayed empty. Art wasn't even sure after all this time how many were left. It might have been just her and Jacks, for all he knew. She recognized Art right away. He assumed it was because of his harelip.

Art asked for Mr. Jackson and was allowed to wait in the familiar tidy hall while Mrs. Lakatos climbed slowly up the stairs, good left leg always first, and then came slowly back down again to say that he could show himself the way. Dion and Bets followed, and Mrs. Lakatos watched them coldly, especially Bets with her long, dirty hair, her unpowdered cheeks and shiny brow, her clothes that were just a touch provocative in the sense that they demonstrated no more interest in hiding her body than they did in making it desirable, revealing the densely freckled shoulder blades, the hair left to grow under her arms. Jacks, big and bald, dressed in a soiled undershirt, met them on the landing. "You ain't been to the house in a long time," he said in his outsized voice. "Normally, I'd be at the factory at this time of day, you know."

"Uncle Jacks, you stopped working there when I was still in junior high. Didn't they close?"

"Right," the big man nodded solemnly. "Otherwise I'd be there now, this time of day."

The only apparent change to the room where Jacks lived was decay. The sagging belly of the bed bowed still further. The two cushions that turned it by day into a sofa that no one ever saw, much less sat on, but that was nevertheless constructed with care each morning, had grown dingier, their lumps more pronounced. Those few spots that Jacks apparently used to the exclusion of all others were rubbed shiny, each an oasis on the accumulated plain of dust, which otherwise covered everything: the chairs he had once tried to sleep on, the windowsill, the top of his small chest of drawers. His few shelves were still empty except for the familiar souvenirs of his army days—the good-conduct medal pinned to the flat green cap, the curling photo of men smiling around a canvas-covered truck—sitting next to the little items colleagues at the factory had given him sometimes for Christmas and the few gifts he had occasionally received in place of affection from the dance-hall girls. Jacks pointed out a little turquoise porcelain poodle sitting at cartoonish attention with a great drooping mustache and a green collar, a figurine that Art had sometimes played with on the nights spent hiding from his father. Jacks blew at its sooty halo, saying, "You used to like him a lot, right, Art?"

"Sure," said Art.

"Hey, you want to keep him?"

"No, Uncle Jacks, thanks. You keep him for me. I don't want to break it." Jacks nodded approvingly at that.

Art sat with Dion and Bets on the bed and looked at Jacks across a room where the changes of the world seemed completely absent and ignored, where even the war was distant and somehow minor. Art felt his family well up within him, wanting desperately to be spoken. Jacks was the only person he had seen since the argument who knew his father, who knew what it meant to be cowed by him and yet for some reason hopeful of the mystical and unknown blessing that was his approval. In that way, it occurred to him now, they were more like brothers, and for a moment he felt almost desperate to talk about the thing they shared, especially when Jacks said suddenly with an attempt at indifference that was as close as he ever came to guile, "So how's your pop? Is he bald like me yet?"

Art felt as if he had passed a test when he managed to say instead that in fact he was there because he needed to talk to his mother, asking if he couldn't have the phone number for Mr. Helms. He was about to offer an explanation, unsure even as he breathed in to fuel his speech if he would tell the truth or not, but Jacks was already nodding and standing and pointing at a pencil mark on the wall by the door, shouting, "I got the number for Helms, yeah. He's my manager, you know, so I got that."

Jacks found an old envelope and wrote it down for him. Art was reluctant to break the spell of relief. He held the slip of paper in his fingers like a talisman, so bewitched he was unable to make the gestures required to leave. There was something too comforting about being in someplace so familiar, and even in a sense for what was the familiar reason: to escape his father. The same room, the same colors; he found even the same sounds as when he had hidden there before, when he had been a child sliding with his toys under the bed

disguised unsuccessfully as a sofa with all around him Jacks'
barrel-shaped voice, reassuring and steady. He sank through
the soft familiarity of it for a moment. Dion had found an old
screen magazine on the bedside table and, as if to fill Art's
silence, he and Jacks were discussing the black-and-white
movie stars, people whose names Art only vaguely recognized,
Claudette Colbert and Jean Harlow. Art listened as he might
to a song in a foreign language until he realized that Bets was
making faces at him that said it was time for them to go.

Jacks had no phone in his room, and Art didn't have the
strength to ask Mrs. Lakatos to use the one in the hall. Art
again politely refused to take the blue poodle, but he hugged
the big man before they headed outside, pressed his face to
the broad sternum like a boat's prow. Dion shook Jacks' hand
and said, "It was very nice to meet you," with a courtesy that
he rarely displayed, even going so far as to call him sir.

When they got outside Dion lit a smoke and said, "Hey,
man, Jacks is beautiful. I could see he really cares about
you, cares about your family. And he's got that natural inno-
cence, right?"

Art said, "I guess," but Dion as always saw straight into
him, and said, "No, that's wrong, Art: don't get hung up like
that. I know people probably look down on him because he's
not so bright, and sure, I mean, obviously that's true, but talking to someone like Jacks—it's like a hotline to reality. Can
you imagine your uncle Jacks in there ever feeding someone
a line? There's no games with a guy like that, no faking, no
scams. Just the truth as best he can understand it, you know.
Nothing else."

When Dion walked ahead, Bets said quietly, "Dion has
a brother—a half brother, really. He's like your uncle Jacks,
only more, if you see what I mean. When we were fighting the

other night, me and Dion, it's because I was trying to convince Dion to head to Canada or Mexico. Well, to go anywhere, really, that isn't jail or Vietnam. But he won't skip out because of his brother. I mean, because he's worried he could never come back, and so he might never see his brother again."

"I didn't know that."

"He doesn't talk about it much."

Art wanted to apologize suddenly for how little he had tried to learn about Dion, or about Bets, really, either. He had somehow thought of them as existing only now, today, without a past, a kind of forever that made them free from the chains of family and history, all the things that on Art hung so heavily that he imagined others could simply sense them, that they were built into his body in the form of his cleft palate, his pale skin that burned in the sun, the limbs that he struggled to control and that never responded with the strength he needed from them. *The puppy doesn't ask questions, it just follows you home,* he thought. All that had mattered was that Dion and Bets were the opposite of what he was, that they were the brave and confident people who occupied the park, who knew people and places, who took him in when he needed to escape his father. Realizing his mistake he felt something like the mixture of disappointment and relief and illumination he had experienced when he first understood, in a moment that was prolonged and vague and yet somehow still sudden, that other people's families took photos, that they looked at them and shared them and kept them in books. Those were books that would never be found in his house because what past his parents had—his father's war, his mother's family—was forgotten by paternal decree, the terrible weight of which could never be shifted. "Does he live with someone, like cousins or something?" he asked Bets. "The brother, I mean."

"That's the worst of it," Bets said. "Dion couldn't take care of him, and it kills him. I think that's why he doesn't like to talk about him. He really did try, you know, but you can't reason with someone like that when he gets worked up. Dion says he's as strong as Hercules. He busted up their apartment a whole bunch of times. They kept having to move because of the landlords, you know. Then I guess he kind of busted Dion up one night. He didn't mean it, but that's how it is. Sometimes intention just doesn't matter. He's in this hospital kind of place now in Maryland. It tears Dion up, you know, thinking of his brother living there, alone. Anyway, I think Jacks reminded him of his brother a bit."

Dion was waving, calling to them. He had found a pay phone.

Art didn't remember passing out. He recalled talking with Mr. Helms and trying to sound confident, even though he was aware Mr. Helms didn't care, that the man just wanted to get to the point and hang up, and afterwards he and Bets and Dion had tried to cut across some empty lots bleached colorless by the summer, where the sun had jumped up at him from the caked flints of glass and the beer-can tabs that studded the ground. Now he was inside where it was cool, lying down on something with vinyl upholstery that stuck to his sweaty face. People talked nearby.

"There's the doctor himself, natch," Dion was saying, "and some pills, maybe an EKG guy, I don't know. Dr. Dodge wants it all up front because there have been guys got their four-F and then kept the dough. What's he going to do, go to the pigs and say, 'Man, these cats didn't pay me for breaking the law'?"

A voice Art didn't recognize said, "And you're sure it's going to work?"

"I'm sure there's a good chance the guy is going to pocket the bread and tell me to go to hell."

"Or Vietnam."

"Right, whichever comes first, or all of the above. Hey, it's not like I'm going to run to the cops either. The Turtle says he's okay, so I'm going to give it a try, but honestly, he could just be planning to take the cash and drive to Mexico."

"It's a popular choice right now," said Bets a little bitterly. Art tried to sit up but somehow it felt instead as if all he did was blink his eyes. When he opened them again he was looking up at a bunch of faces, Bets and Dion and someone else, and Dion was smiling at him, saying, "Hey, brother, that was almost cool, the way you went down, you know? Like you were dancing." He helped Art into a sitting position. They were in a semicircular diner booth with a metal-rimmed table. "Did you eat anything today?"

"What kind of dance?" Art asked, and Dion laughed, not his usual cursory noise of appreciation, but a real laugh, the kind that your body gives you, and it made Art happy to think he had done that because Dion, who was always amusing other people, hardly ever laughed himself, even before the lottery and the low number and the gnawing worry. Dion said, "Let's get you something, like some toast and a coffee, I guess?"

"Where are we?"

"The Reverend Mother's," Bets said coldly.

"What's that?"

"Man, Reverend Mom's is like a holy rite of passage," said Dion. "I thought this was your old neighborhood."

"It's a soup kitchen," said Bets, "for people who could mostly afford their own soup."

"I don't want soup," said Art, shaking his head, and Dion laughed again.

"I didn't want to come here," Bets told Art while Dion

went off in search of food. "But Dion was the one carrying you, and we were close, so here we are. You should be more careful to eat, baby." She ran a hand down his face.

Dion came back followed by a small barefoot woman. She was wearing a flimsy dress, her wrists and ankles buried in bracelets, long hair swinging almost to her waist. She talked as she stepped through the group of men seated on the floor, her voice strident and purposeful and hectoring. At some point in her speech, she put a tray down in front of Art. He could see her bare breasts inside her dress as she bent over, and he tried not to look but he felt as if there was no strength in him at all. She was still talking when she left. The tray held coffee in a chipped cup, and a plate with two pieces of buttered toast, some jam in a little plastic cup, and a spoon filled with peanut butter.

Art started to eat. The moment he did, he felt better, but immediately he was overwhelmed with a sudden worry that he had dreamed of Bets and Dion in his faint, that somehow his desires had risen to the untended surface. It was like the feeling that he sometimes had after a lot of weed, that others around him could know his thoughts, but far worse, because in his moment of oblivion he might easily have told them what he was thinking or imagining out loud, himself, no telepathy required, a blast of self-incrimination—and how afterwards could he know? Had he floated across his unconscious back to the morning before the lottery, when he had stood looking through the doorless hole to their bedroom where Bets sat on top of Dion, her breasts dipping through the thin slice of daybreak that lay between them?

Art had been completely unable to look away, filled with desire but also with fear at what noise he might make in trying to move back, so he had remained suspended there, breathless, enthralled, scared that one of them would turn in his direction, but captivated. The memory of them invaded his dreams, joining the naked body from his parents' room, his father's lover and the summit of the old man's hypocrisy: the hard-breasted woman who against his wishes had occupied his dream life for so long already. Any of this might have been mumbled or screamed or moaned as he lay unconscious in Dion's arms; he couldn't be sure.

Dion tried to move the leather bag Bets carried from its place by her side in the little booth, but she pulled it away from him and slipped it behind her back to make space for him instead. "You still know what's what?" said Dion as he sat down. "Or do we need to call that Helms again?"

Art offered him the paper from his jeans pocket, on one side the information Jacks had given them in numbers that looked like the blocks a child might draw, on the other in Art's own tiny, self-conscious writing a pair of addresses. Art pointed to the first address. "That's the one where she was when I called, but her second shift is at this one. She's going to be leaving the first place by twelve-thirty, he said, so I guess where we go depends on what time it is."

Dion checked a naked wrist. "Half past a freckle, my friend. Let's find out." To someone sitting nearby he said, "Hey, man, what time is it?"

The man shrugged and said, "Reverend Mother doesn't have any clocks."

"Right, sure. Anybody else?" Dion said, looking around. "Anyone know the time?" He looked at the men cross-legged or reclining on the floor. "Any of you guys?"

A man in a soiled white collarless shirt and cutoff jeans was sitting in the lotus position, his back very straight, his eyes closed. Without opening them, he said, "I'm late, you're late. It's just one more plan to divide and conquer, and I refuse to play their game. It's just like money, man."

Then they were all at it. "That's right," someone said. "I'd rather have a piece of paper with a poem on it or something than a portrait of some old slave owner. That has more value to me."

"Like, hey brother, can you spare a Byron?"

"Who has change for a Walt Whitman?"

"This is why I don't like Reverend Mom's," said Bets quietly to Art. "All these middle-class white kids at a hippie theme park." She bent over her purse and dug around.

"What about you, man?" said Dion to one of the others. "You have a watch?"

"I had one, brother, but I threw it away. I just couldn't deal with that kind of pressure."

Bets sat up in the booth with one hand held high over her head and said in a loud voice, serious almost to the point of anger but still with a hint of her sweet, triumphant mockery, "I will give all the shake left in this dime bag to whoever can tell me the fucking time."

At 12:57 they left for the place where Art's mother was starting her second shift of the day.

•

Bets said it was easiest to cross back the way they had come. There was a bus that stopped near the boardinghouse; it would take them in the right direction. They walked again into the old neighborhood, Art hanging behind the others, still harried by the fear that he might have said something he shouldn't during those missed moments when Dion had carried him in his arms, the longed-for embrace unseen and unfelt. At home he knew that he would talk in his sleep, the running brook of his ideas heard gurgling through his throat, and he had sometimes woken up to his father drunkenly demanding he repeat himself. Of course Art never even knew he was speaking, so for his father's sake he would invent what he might have said, talking about school or something the neighbors had told his mother until the old man grew bored and wandered off to comfort himself with the sound of ice cracking in tepid liquor.

Over the ten minutes or so of their walk the anxiety of the idea that he might have spoken spread to anything else Art would think of, so that a thin fear ran through him when someone outside the Italian butcher's recognized him and raised a hand in greeting. As they crossed the street where the boardinghouse stood, Art hoped that they wouldn't run into Jacks: it was as if a second visit would trigger some unnamed problem they had magically avoided the first time, might somehow undermine the perfect kindliness of their earlier good-byes, call to the surface all the words that lurked in his sleeping mind. He wondered if he could see Jacks again and still maintain his silence about his father.

It wasn't that fighting with his father was anything unusual, a sudden change. In that way, it wasn't even really an event, no different from the rest of their interaction except in scope—a louder, more virulent version of the conversation Art believed they were engaged in all the time, whether together or apart. The real difference was that Art, maybe encouraged by the knowledge that Bets and Dion waited for him, that he had a kind of home with them when this one was taken from him or he gave it up, whichever it was, had at last spoken up for himself. He had turned the question of guilt and virtue around so that for once it faced his father, for once it reflected not Art's weakness and inadequacy, but his father's false claims, his reliance on his wife's income, and above all his duplicity. How long had Art been waiting to confront his father with this, the knowledge of the other woman, the one who had taken his affection from them, who had stood naked in their home? Dion and Bets had set this budding urge against his fear, an urge based on their conviction that honesty would lead to freedom, that he should accept the need, should confront his father.

The bus stop was on a busy block. There were shops with faded signs up and down both sides of the street, and stoops where old men sat in their undershirts and stared at the passing traffic. Dion talked a pair of girls wearing almost identical outfits of tight sleeveless T-shirts and flares into slipping him their transfers. A bus pulled in and they got on. One of the girls handed the transfers to Dion out the window, the papers flapping like little flags, Dion running alongside to snatch them from her tiny fingers. It was always amazing to Art to see how people gave him their trust, the attention that seemed by nature to be his, the unenvious, heartfelt acceptance that even strangers laid on him like a leafy crown. Art was filled again with admiration and yearning, the strange feeling he had of wanting not just Dion's notice, not just his love, but to have Dion within him, to be the other person so unlike the one he had been trapped in.

Dion half jogged, half danced his way back to them, waving the long slips of yellow and white paper, one in each hand. To Art he said, "You look better. You went completely white before."

"What color am I now?"

Dion patted him on the shoulder. "The usual, man," he said, "just, you know, Art color." He lit a cigarette and said,

"Bets told you about my brother, she said." Art nodded. Dion nodded, too, and Art tried to think of something he could ask him, but then he saw in his face that Dion was gone again, distracted by his swift-running fears. Dion followed his thoughts out into the road, and stared out past them at the long tube of hot tarmac in search of their bus.

Art looked over at his reflection in the glass of the bus shelter: laid like a ghost over the people on the other side of the partition was the stringy, unwashed hair, the limp arms falling like sausage links from the short sleeves, the triangle of flat chest, hairless and slightly sunburnt, and on it the necklace of wood and braided leather Bets had made for him. There were wet spots around his armpits and under his belt, and his face was shiny with sweat, beads that set off one after another on the slow journey to his neck. In the middle of it all, barely visible in the spectral vision but as evident to him as a flashing light, sat the rupture: warped mouth and nose, the right nostril flaring above the curled lip, the emblems of his body's treachery.

Bets appeared over his shoulder and smiled at him, a face of kindness and sympathy. He made up his mind to ask her. "Did I say anything while I was out or unconscious or whatever?"

"You were so quiet I worried for a second you weren't breathing."

"That's good," said Art.

Bets almost laughed. "Baby, somehow only you would think thàt was good," she told him. Then Dion was with them, saying, "Heads up, boys and girls, this is us." The bus rolled in.

As they climbed the steep steps Bets said to Art, "They're not wrong, you know, those guys at Mom's. About money and time and all the rest of it. But so what? Talk like that isn't what's going to keep Dion out of the army, sitting around saying the system shouldn't be what it is. People who shout about how they don't recognize the authority of the court still wind up in jail, you know what I mean?" But suddenly Art wasn't listening any more, because through the window of the bus he found himself looking straight at his father, the old man looking back at him from the driver's seat of a truck facing the other direction. Art would have run if he could, but there was nowhere to go, so instead he stood where he was, completely still. They stared at each other blankly for a moment until the bus pulled away. He was aware suddenly of his heart, how it shuddered and bumped against his ribs.

·

Their fight had come all at once, irrepressible: there had been the old man, rummaging for lost change and someone else's hoarded savings but with the righteousness of a landlord assessing his estates, imperious somehow even as he dropped to his knees to sweep an arm through the dusty cupboard. He had cursed at Art, and then cursed Art's absent mother, the woman he had used and cheated on, the woman who was at that moment working the job that kept the old man stocked with gin. Within Art stirred the thought that had long been kicking for delivery, the thing he had always fought down because, however much he wanted to express it, expel it, he could see it only in the color of his own complicity: because he, too, had lusted for the ungenerous, the hard and foreign body glimpsed from the bed's perilous underdark, desires that terrified him most because they were shared, however unaware the partner.

Art felt in that moment as if he had waited for years with the exact words stored and macerating somewhere just below his gut, and once he had accepted finally to release them they bubbled out suddenly and in a voice that jerked and trembled, ran far beyond its owner's control: "Don't talk about her like that."

"You don't tell me what to do, not under my roof." His father spoke almost indifferently, busy pushing aside the small and fragile things Art's mother cherished in keeping hidden, the cups and saucers, the glasses, which rattled weakly.

"Your roof? Where do you learn this stuff?" Art became aware as he spoke that he was screaming, his tone stretched and fraying. He tried to make himself sound reasonable, but it was impossible: his voice was no longer his own. It belonged instead to the hysteria of his emotion, and so he bleated like a farm animal: "It's like there's some kind of handbook full of these ridiculous sayings for . . . for shitty fathers." His father looked up at that, and Art had an inconceivable feeling. It mixed fear with pleasure, stirred together the satisfaction of having pierced the tin shell of his father's indifference with alarm at what perhaps waited inside. He wanted to stop, but also to go on, and stopping now seemed impossible, so he fell forward into his own words. "And anyway," he bleated, "anyway, who are you kidding? How is anything here yours, you know? Ma pays for it all. Ma does all the work."

Was that when his father had stood, small and dense and full of quiet menace? Was that when Art had noticed that the sofa stood between them, a hurdle that protected him? Art's father said, "I'm going to tell you something that you don't know. Without me, your mother would be nothing. Men paid to rub against her and call it dancing. For a nickel, she was doing that, with strangers, for nothing more than a nickel.

Girls like that, Jesus. You think the world loves a girl like that? Without me, your mother would be nothing, and you would be nothing. I made this family. You owe me everything."

"What the hell do you do around here except drink and . . . and . . ." Art found himself crying, scared of his own sudden desire to hurt but unable to hold back the emerging thing until at last the simplicity of it slipped through his mouth like a yolk cracked loose from an egg: "and lie."

Abe's head jerked suddenly. It was the first time in his whole life that Art remembered seeing the hard coating of his father's expression change so drastically or so fast. When Art didn't answer, the old man made a gesture with his hand as if he were moving some invisible curtain out of the way, and demanded again, louder this time, "What the hell are you talking about?"

Art, his mind full of the woman, his father's secret lover, who had walked naked in his parents' home, screamed back at him finally, his face straining and his throat caught in a tourniquet of effort: "That's right, lie. And you think nobody knows, you think you have everyone fooled," he went on. "But not me. Because I'm not blind. I'm not fucking blind."

"What are you talking about?" his father asked. "You little bastard, tell me what the hell you're talking about, you lying little piece of shit."

"Do you know I once saw you?" Art yelled. "Do you know that I was there once, in your bedroom? I was there, and I saw." The words were a strangled croaking now, his body was so full of fear and rage and the painful relief of his silence finally bursting, and they shook and trembled as they left him but he said them again if for no other reason than because he couldn't stop the flood once it was unleashed, screaming over and over, "I saw, and I know," and he could tell that his father had understood him because the old man's face turned a sudden bloodless white, his lips pressed together so hard they almost disappeared. For a moment the two of them were both quiet and still, the only noise the heavy movement of sobbed breath through Art's open mouth, the old man's broken face hanging silent on the twitching head. Then Art ran while his father screamed after him. If any of the sounds the old man made were words, Art didn't hear them.

Jimmy had been talking again. Kunstler wished he would go back to reading his book, but he wouldn't keep his eyes off the map for longer than a minute now, always looking for the shortest route to the next drop-off. Kunstler wouldn't be able to make an easy detour to the apartment to look through the boy's things with Jimmy pretending he was a native guide, and it made him anxious, edgy. "Do you even know what's in any of the boxes?" Jimmy asked. "I mean, do you ever read the bill of lading, or even just the stuff written on them? Right there, on the boxes, in big letters? Company names and stuff. What I'm asking is, do you have any idea what it really is you do for a living? On the days you bother to show up, I mean. I'm just curious is the thing. Be ready to take the second right."

"What?" said Kunstler. His hand hurt, and his foot hurt, too. Jimmy had found him an aspirin but it wasn't doing anything, and the measly half cup of ice the deli guy had been barely willing to part with had melted almost immediately. The returning pain after the brief numbing was worse than before. He didn't need a reminder any more, he needed a drink—but he had emptied the plastic flask of gin to take the aspirin when Jimmy wasn't looking. It all made him tired: the pain and the heat and Jimmy's endless noise. If he couldn't get a drink, he had wondered, maybe he could find a moment to sleep. He needed a clear head to think about the boy, only now this sudden fatigue had crawled over him, captured him like a net. It was pulling him down, and while they waited for the light he even thought maybe he had nodded off.

That was why at first he didn't understand that it wasn't a dream, that he really was looking at the boy in the sky, looking right at him. His face was floating in the sun only four or maybe five feet away and between them a cascade of reflections, layers of glass echoing glass, Abe's own mirror and windshield and half-rolled window reflected in the window of a stopped bus, images shared back and forth of the city around them, of cars moving and people walking, of Kunstler's own face. In the middle of all that, looking out through the captured spray of white sun, was the blank, still face of the boy standing on a bus, one limp arm raised to hold the strap. Kunstler stared, and the face stared right back. Jimmy's voice was a blur in the background, the cars piling up in his side-view, all of it unimportant when he understood that he had done it: he had found the boy. Kunstler almost smiled. In amazement he looked, and the boy looked back, stared directly into his eyes, until, with a gentle sideward roll, the bus pulled away.

"Abe, man, that's you they're honking at. Let's go. The light doesn't get any greener than this."

"No, no," said Kunstler. "Shit." He threw open his door. His sleeve caught on the window crank and ripped, and he nearly fell out of the cab onto the road as he twisted to face the back of the departing bus. There was no way to follow but to run tripping up the moonscape of patched tarmac between the two lanes of traffic, the bus moving farther away with every step. Cars slid past him on his right while from his left drivers trapped behind the truck yelled insults, but he kept running. A cab door sprang open and Kunstler had to duck around the angry driver. He ran on for as long as he could, foot pounding after foot until he was caught short, breathless, cut and doubled by a stitch across his gut. The bus drove on, unhurried, the taillights flashing red for one insincere second before it picked up speed. He stood there and watched it go, hunched over, his throbbing thumb tucked into his armpit, heaving for breath through the sweat that collected along his lip. He recalled unbidden the basement furnace, shrouded in its own heat.

Kunstler blinked hard, then walked slowly back up the middle of the road, limping a little. He had run farther than he thought, and it was a long way to the bus stop. Jimmy had pulled the truck over on the other side of the street, and Abe had to wait for the long backlog of cars to pass him, some of the drivers giving him the finger as they went by. When he finally got across, Jimmy was still in the driver's seat.

"Twist your ankle?" Jimmy called down to him through the window. "It serves you right, running out in the road like a looney. What the hell is wrong with you? Come around."

Abe didn't move. "What do you mean?"

"I mean you're *pazzo* in the head. What, did you see a pretty girl? Trust me, they're not worth it. Now come on around, man. Let's go."

"Around? No."

"Yeah," said Jimmy. "I'm driving. Like you told me, you're too tired or whatever. I figure more whatever than tired, you know what I mean?" He pulled the empty gin bottle out of the driver's door pocket and tossed it down to Abe, who caught and held it in his good hand without looking at it. "Now come on around, get in. We have to go. I'm trying to salvage something of our route so those assholes upstairs don't fine us a day's pay."

"No," said Abe. "I have to drive. We have to turn around, go that way." He started to open the cab door. Jimmy pulled it shut again, and said in a tight tone, "Abe, you have to go around and get in on the other side. Then I am going to drive this fucking truck in that fucking direction, towards our next fucking delivery. You can come or not. Last chance."

Jimmy tried to get ready to leave. He ground the gears and turned away for a second to look at the shift. That's when Kunstler opened the door, grabbed Jimmy's leg, and pulled him out of his seat. They fell on top of each other on the tarmac. Several cars started honking and someone yelled. Neither would let the other go, so they stayed there, elbows and knees knocking on the pavement as they rolled. Jimmy finally managed to get free and stand up. He pushed Kunstler away, but when he turned to get back in the truck Kunstler stood, too, and beat Jimmy hard on the back of the head with an object he found in his hand: the empty plastic bottle, three blows each making a tiny popping noise. Jimmy turned and punched him in the gut, and Kunstler fell to one knee.

Jimmy looked at him for a moment with a face full of surprise and confusion, one hand set tenderly on the back of his head. Then he climbed into the cab. "This is my fucking job," he yelled, grinding the gears again. "This is where I work. You asshole piece of shit." He finally found first, and the truck jerked out onto the road and stalled. Jimmy fought with the ignition until the truck shuddered to life again. He yelled, "You go too far, Abe. Too goddamn far. The hell with you." The truck pulled away. Kunstler managed finally to stand straight and turned to the people across the street at the bus stop. "Where does that bus go?" he tried to ask, "the one that left? I need to know what number it was," but his wind was gone and he could barely even hear himself, so nobody answered.

A man right beside Kunstler said, "Oh, my god. Yes, I thought it was you. What's going on?" Kunstler gave a start and backed away from him a step and so nearly tripped on the curb behind them. The man put out a steadying hand and when they were arm in arm said, "Are you all right? That man, the truck . . . you want me to call the police?"

"What? No." Kunstler looked up the road again, the other way, to where the bus had gone, then back to the man. He was still having trouble breathing and his voice was a tiny hiss. "No. Who are you?"

"I'm Arnie. The French cleaner? Over here. I used to do your suits."

"You used to?" Kunstler said.

"Right." The man was still holding him.

"My suits?" Kunstler said.

"Right." The man smiled and nodded and so Kunstler nodded, too, carefully. He looked at the man who called himself Arnie. He was a skinny guy, older, an open bald crown behind a greased-down tentacle of grey hair, liver spots like a handful of tossed pennies. He wore glasses. Kunstler thought, *Whoever he is, I can beat him if I have to.* Kunstler said to him, "Do you know what bus that was, what number?" The guy had to lean close to hear him.

"That left? Well, there's three or four buses stop here. You remember."

"No," Kunstler admitted weakly. "I don't." He looked for the first time at the buildings around him.

The man said, "Yes, it's been some time since I've seen you around the neighborhood, years maybe. And of course it looks different now. Are you all right?" Kunstler knew he wanted to think about something, something about the boy, and the appearance here of someone who seemed to know who he was, but the fight and the heat and the lack of gin and the man's talking seemed to make it hard for him to think. His knees felt soft, watery. He must have looked unsteady because the man said, "Do you want to sit down?"

"No," said Kunstler. "I'm fine"—but still he let the man lead him a few yards to a storefront. A bell hanging on the door rang when they entered.

It was cooler inside. A fan swung its slow, buzzing blue plastic head from side to side. There was a padded stool and a large sewing machine at a workstation inside the shop-front window and Arnie directed him to sit there. A pair of pants were on the table, and Kunstler knew without wanting to that they were being let out at the waist. A boy with a little alligator on his shirt was standing behind the counter.

"We have an old customer here," said Arnie. "Forgive me, I don't remember your name."

Kunstler was still trying to think of something, but it wouldn't come. He said, "Do you have something to drink?"

"Oh, of course. Dennis, Mr., uh . . . had an accident outside. Would you get him a glass of water?"

"What?" said Kunstler. "No, not water. Something to drink." He made the motion with his hand of lifting a glass. He found he was still holding the little plastic bottle. He moved it to his other hand, his claw. "A drink."

"Oh, you mean a . . . ? Well, not here, no. I suppose they might have a beer at the deli." He hesitated and then handed the kid a bill from his pocket. "Dennis, run and get Mr., uh . . .

Run and get a beer from Mr. Mileski. My sister's boy," he said to Kunstler when the kid had ducked under the counter and out the door to the sound of the bell. Kunstler slipped the empty plastic bottle between the stool and his thigh. "He's helping me out this weekend. Or I'm helping her out, looking after him. Once someone gets a family, everyone they've ever met is a babysitter, but of course you know how that is. And it's nice to have him around, he's a good kid." He waited for a moment, but when Kunstler didn't say anything, he went on. "Yours must be even older now, I would think. I don't remember his name, forgive me, but I remember him, or at least, I remember one thing."

He took off his glasses, and from his pocket produced a cloth. He wiped the sweat from his nose and from inside the bridge of the heavy black plastic frames before starting on the lenses. *It's good he took those off,* Kunstler thought, *that way they won't break when I hit him for talking about the boy's face.*

Instead Arnie said, "He was always so serious when he ran errands for his mother. Do you know, he used to count your clothes when I gave them back to him. It really struck me. It was so . . ." He looked around with his blind eyes for the word, and produced it finally with a flourish of his hands like a magician: "Meticulous," he said. "I mean, for someone so young, to be so careful," and with that returned his glasses to their place. "So vigilant. I remember that very well."

"He was just here," Kunstler said, motioning vaguely. "He left on that bus."

"Did he? Well. Is he doing all right? Is he in school? Oh, here's Dennis." The bell rang again and the kid came back in. He carefully handed a can and some change to Arnie, and Arnie handed the can to Kunstler. The kid went back to his place behind the counter. "Were the two of you visiting old neighborhood friends? And may I ask what happened with that man?" Arnie said, and again Kunstler knew he needed to focus on what it was he was trying to remember. The kid must have been staring at Kunstler's crippled hand, because when Kunstler looked over at him, he turned quickly away.

Kunstler opened the can and drank his beer, the whole can as fast as he could. Right away the bubbles burned and choked him, but he wouldn't slow. Beer ran down his chin and onto his shirt and was absorbed by the bandage and still he didn't stop, but leaned his head back farther and with held breath let his throat open and contract, fought the panic by thinking, *This is what it does, trust the mechanism to do its work,* and even as it hurt he appreciated this feeling of being pulled inside himself, alone with his body for just a moment, seized by his own flesh. He knew the old man and the kid were watching him in something like dismay, but he needed to think straight and a beer taken in sips would never give him the power.

The whole beer helped, though, because when it was done he was able suddenly to see. The man was right: he had been here, he knew this place from before the accident and the end of the factory, he had passed these buildings each day in the car on the way to work, had walked right here with his girl on Sundays to go to the park, or to the bars at night, in the days before the boy came, when things were good. It was almost as if he could look out the dry cleaner's plate-glass window and see himself driving down the street, the car sliding past the same stoops and storefronts, the shop signs moving easily by, shutters rolling open as the day began. He held the steering wheel with two loose fingers, and let his left foot gently ride the clutch. The early morning road was open and inviting,

and the factory waited at the end of the ride like an orna-
ment. Meanwhile, there beside him in the passenger seat,
knees against the dash, his breathing audible even over the
steady, regal hum of the engine, blissfully unaware of his own
imbecility, big and thick and restless as an animal, sat Jacks.

Kunstler stood up at the thought. Jacks lived here. He
could have seen the boy. What might the boy have told him?
"Yes," he said to the puzzled-looking man, who was running
a palm over the big empty space of his skull. "Old neighborhood friends." It was the only thing that made any sense—
and if the boy had said something to Jacks, well: the big fool
might say anything, to anyone. He had to find out.

The bell rang as Kunstler stepped out onto the hot sidewalk and was immediately gripped by a fist of wet air and the
smell of garbage. The buildings were still coming into focus,
but he knew them well enough now. The beer can was in his
hand, he realized, the pull tab hanging from a finger on the
other—which meant the empty bottle was sitting on the stool
in the dry cleaner. Kunstler dropped the can and the tab on
the sidewalk and turned in the direction of the lodging house
where Jacks had lived. He had only gone a few steps before he
started to run.

·

The uptight little land-lady in her schoolmarm clothes
pretended at first not to know who he was. Kunstler could
tell from her sour pout that she recognized him, though. "She
keeps the vintage bile in the cellar for when her lodgers have
guests," he used to say about her, and he easily imagined there
was no guest she liked less than Abe Kunstler, who didn't go

to church or wipe his feet, who kept his hat on indoors and wasn't polite—a guest who, when he came to her door, which was something he wanted to do about as much as she wanted to have it done, was usually not even sober. She would lie to him that the boy and his mother weren't there when he knew damn well they were, because where else were they going to be, but he would let it go if only because he could tell she was itching for an excuse to call the police, her finger was practically in the dial every time she spoke, and even at his drunkest he knew what to avoid.

This time she pretended for a second not to know who he meant when he asked for Jacks, but maybe she had sensed his desperation, or even something else within him, something for which the dirt and the breathlessness were a sign that penetrated even her posturing rectitude, because she didn't pretend long. Still she made it a point to inform him that *Mr. Jackson* wasn't in, that *Mr. Jackson* had left maybe a few minutes before, was maybe heading that way, around the corner and up the block, but really how was she supposed to know where *Mr. Jackson* was going? This time she told him the truth, at least: once he turned the corner Kunstler could see Jacks lumbering a block or so ahead. He pursued at a slow, limping run that still left him so out of breath he didn't speak when he reached Jacks, just grabbed the larger man by the elbow.

"Hey, Abe," said Jacks. "Hey, I was just thinking about you before. It's been a long time. Hey, look at that, will you, you still have all your hair. None of the guys have all their hair no more but you. Blackie always said you age half as slow as the rest of us, remember? You told him it was 'clean living.' That made me laugh. You were having a drink, and we were all pretty gone, that's why it was so funny. We were at that bar."

"Sure," Kunstler said. He was winded, and had bent up to make the breathing easier. He wiped his face with his bad hand.

"Say, did you have a accident?" Kunstler looked at his claw and then dumbly back up at Jacks, who started to pat ineffectually at Abe's clothes. "Look at you, you got blood, looks like, and you're all dirty, and here you got a rip. You always was the most best-dressed guy at the factory, I guess, but here you are now, you look like you fell down a well. That's what my mother used to say to me when I got dirty when I was a kid. Even if I wasn't wet, like you're not wet." Jacks laughed. "Really, though, are you okay?"

Kunstler waved at Jacks to lay off rubbing at him using the tight little movements of a man chasing away a bee. "What do you think?" he panted. "That I cut myself shaving?"

Jacks looked at him with tilted head and then chuckled. "You still tell good jokes."

"Fine," said Kunstler. "Jacks, the boy. Did you see him?"

"Who?"

Kunstler struggled to stay calm. "The boy, you . . . Did you see the boy, did he come and talk to you?"

"Art, you mean?"

"Yes, him, the . . . Art, yes. Have you seen him?"

"Yeah, I saw him. He came to the house, and him and his friends visited me in my room for a while. His friend knew all about the good actresses, you know, from the old talkies."

"Did he tell you anything? What did he say?"

"He said Jean Harlow should have been a bigger star, if only she hadn't have died."

"What?"

"I think so, too."

"No, Jacks, not the friend. What did the boy . . . what did Art say? He came to see you. Why did he come to see you?"

"Oh. He was looking for his mom."

Kunstler gave a long groan. "He's looking for her? Shit. Has she been around here?"

"No. But I had the number for Helms."

Kunstler thought, *If there was a button I could press that would shoot him into outer space right now, I guess I would push it,* but he only said, "What does that mean, Jacks, the number for Helms?"

"Art needed to find his mom and so he asked for the phone number for Mr. Helms. And I have his number because he's our supervisor, so I gave it to Art so he could find out where she was working today."

"A telephone number for the cleaning company? Okay, I need that. I need that number. Anything you gave him, I need. You have the number on you? No? Back at your place?"

"You're looking for Inez, too?"

"Yes. For both of them. It's important. Do you know where she is?"

"No. But Mr. Helms knows. Is everything all right? Don't you have his number at your place?"

"Let's just get a move on."

They walked back to the lodging house, the little limping man and the big lumbering one, Jacks talking the whole time, Kunstler trying to hurry them. Kunstler waited around the side of the brick house to steal the tiny bit of shade it hoarded down its wall and hoped the old lady wouldn't spot him and come offer more grief while Jacks went in to get the number. Kunstler heard the smooth easy sound of cars driving by in the distance and nearby some birds making a racket. There was still the important thing he had to ask Jacks and he wished he could have a drink to do it on. He didn't know what he would do about the answer. He found he was thinking about the sharp knife from the kitchen; he shook the thoughts away, and told himself the oppressive heat had leaked into his mind.

The nail had gone completely black on his swollen, throbbing thumb. Squeezing the knuckle with his other hand seemed to relieve the pressure a little so he did that while he walked back and forth in a tight circle beside the lodging house and wondered where he had lost his cigarettes. Running had shifted his bandages and he really needed to fix them, but he wasn't going to ask to use the bathroom at Jacks' place. When Jacks finally came back he said, "Jesus Christ. Did you get lost?"

"Sorry, Abe, I had to talk with Mrs. Lakatos."

"Sure. I should have guessed she'd have you in for lunch when she knows I'm waiting."

"It wasn't for lunch."

"I know it wasn't." Jacks was toying with a slip of paper, and Kunstler yanked it away from him. He turned his face towards the paper but didn't really look at it. Instead he tensed up, his whole body suddenly taut and sprung, and said, "Okay. Listen now, Jacks. This is important. Let me ask you something. What else did he say, what else did the boy say? Art?"

"What do you mean?"

"God damn it, Jacks. Do you know that talking to you sometimes is a good argument for gun laws? I mean what other God damn words came out of his mouth, is what I mean. I mean did he talk about me? Did he tell you anything about me?"

"No," said Jacks simply in his dull bellow.

"You're sure? He didn't say anything about me when he was talking about trying to find his mother?"

"No. He didn't say nothing about you."

Kunstler relaxed a little and looked back down at the slip of paper. "Is that a four or a nine?" he demanded.

"That's a four. Say, Abe, do you want a clean shirt? I could bring you one of mine."

Kunstler looked at his own ruined clothes, but when he imagined himself floating through the city in one of Jacks' huge things like a nightshirt or worse he said, "I guess not. At least I know what I look like in mine. There's no telling what they might mistake me for in one of yours. Which way to a pay phone?"

Kunstler started out at a limping trot and Jacks called after him. "See you, Abe!" He called it again—"See you! See you round!"—so that finally Kunstler turned and gave him a wave. He decided that the minute he could he would have to find a drink.

It wasn't that the guard was lonely. On weekend shifts, as a rule, he barely said three words to anybody, and that was exactly why he took as many weekend shifts as he could— which was plenty, since no one else wanted them. The building was practically an empty shell from Friday night to Monday morning, one in a series of empty shells that made up the small office district, echoing and unvisited, a kind of graveyard where they buried all the man-hours that had died in them during the week. After college he had worked in an office for a short time that had still been much too long, and he thought of it frankly as a form of death. Maybe even better would have been to call it a form of murder that was also somehow suicide: people killing one another and themselves to be the ones who stayed latest and did the most of a thing that wasn't important to any of them in the first place, or at least had never been important to him. He understood that in their minds they had mostly worked themselves to death for promotions, but it was hard to see the point in that because as far as he could tell his boss and the man above him had been even more anxious and unhappy than anyone. *There has to be somebody somewhere getting a hell of a deal out of all this,* he told himself, *but I'll never meet him, and I won't like him if I do.*

He had taken the job for exactly the same reason he had gone to college: because people told him it was a good opportunity, the kind of thing a solidly middle-class young man did to "get ahead in the world," which was the other thing solidly middle-class young men did. From almost the minute he sat down at his desk on his first day he wanted out. Not just out of the company where he worked, but out of all companies, all offices, with their quasi-royal executives building fiefdoms out of carbon paper and mimeo ink. He wanted out so much he was stupid enough to join the army to get it.

Now about once a month he told his sister on the telephone how odd he still found it that it had been the army and the time he spent in Korea, every minute of which he hated, that made him understand how much he hated everything that had come before it, too, when you would have expected him to think fondly of anything that wasn't the war.

Of course his sister didn't want to hear about it, because her husband, who had never been in the army, thought going to Korea had been a fantastic and patriotic thing to do for people who weren't too busy making a lot of money the way he had been, and apparently that kind of stupidity was contagious. Although the guard didn't like to admit it, that was actually one of the reasons he insisted on talking about it, on repeating to her how the idea of living through hell only to find himself back at work in an office, well: the idea made him sick. It seemed insane—even sinful, somehow.

One night when he was on a really impressive R & R bender in Tokyo he admitted this sin to a fat corporal who asked him what he would prefer to do, if he hated working in an office so much. He didn't ask in the sarcastic way most people seemed to, the one that assumed the answer would be a blank face and a shrug because there was nothing possible to say. The corporal had been honestly curious, asking with the real, almost tender inquisitiveness the guard had only ever found in people who were pretty much pickled in alcohol.

The guard was shocked and dimly angry when he realized he wasn't sure of the answer. No one had ever asked him before. Worse, he had never asked himself, and he was aware suddenly in the extravagant way drinking makes you aware that it might have been years before he got around to considering it so straightforwardly if not for Korea. It almost made him angry to think he might get something good out of the war after all, but he set that aside for the moment and tried to approach the question carefully, with respect and thoroughness, both amplified by the next round, which meant he took a long time answering. In the end, although the corporal wasn't awake any more to hear the answer, the guard had decided that he liked bebop jazz, and the books he had been made to read in his literature classes at college, and building things in the garage. Sometimes he liked camping or hiking (but not fishing). Above all he liked to have company when it suited him and the rest of the time to be let alone, and wanted to have a job where no one expected him to get excited about shaving soap or elastic or whatever it was they were selling or to smile at people he didn't like.

When they cleverly ended the war without anyone bothering first to win it, he came back and started searching for something that suited him better than the office had. The forestry service had been too isolated, and he realized he preferred to be someplace where he could sit on a bar stool and talk to someone if he felt like it, but driving a taxi involved dealing with too many strangers, trying to keep them happy.

One night in a jazz club he learned from the guy next to him at the bar that having shot a gun in blind panic fifteen years earlier pretty much entitled him to a job where he wouldn't have to do much and what he did have to do could happen weekends and nights when no one was around, a job where promotions didn't exist to worry about, and no one wanted to talk to you about anything. He thought it seemed like a good deal, so he became a security guard. Because it was the weekend, the building and the neighborhood were empty. To the guard it seemed it would be only right if the whole city turned out empty on a day hot as that, when anyone with half a brain should be heading to the shore. All you needed was a few bucks and a towel and you could get some relief. It was even better for him: he would go on Tuesday, when only the tourists and some schoolkids would be there and all the local working stiffs had gone back to killing themselves for someone else. Although right now he was trapped in a wash-and-wear uniform that made him stream with sweat, he supposed he might eventually be the only gainfully employed man in Trenton who would actually have found enough space on the beach that week to lie down flat without having his foot in someone else's coleslaw.

Even on the weekends, though, people passing through to other places came into the building sometimes because they needed directions or a bathroom. If it was directions, he gave them as best he could. If they wanted the bathroom, he would say, "You and me both, buddy," and that was generally the whole of it, because while he had access to the one in the dentist's office on the ground floor, he wasn't allowed to let other people in there, and wasn't about to explain all that to them. So he wasn't surprised that they came in, because they could have wanted directions, or the john. What surprised the guard was that despite their intrusion on his solitude, he had been happy to see them. Not the man, that is: the kids. He thought it was something like the way city people are happy when they go on a drive and come across deer grazing or a butterfly shows up on the windowsill: a little glimpse into a world you don't usually get to see. These kids weren't going to get jobs in offices doing things they didn't care about, and they certainly weren't going to join the army and kill people they didn't know for just about any reason anyone could think to tell them, which meant they already knew what it had taken him three years in an office and a tour of duty in Asia to learn.

When they pushed through the doors he gently dropped the book he was reading into the open drawer and put his hands on the desk and tried to appear official, which was pretty much all the job ever consisted of. It was hot enough that he didn't bother to put on his cap, although he should have. He already had the epaulettes and the gaudy alloy badge, and he had clipped in the uniform tie despite the weather. The kids stood there for a moment looking uncertain of themselves. It occurred to the guard that they were wearing their own uniform: variations on a T-shirt above low-slung jeans that were tight until the knee and then splayed out like the leg on a draft horse. He could almost imagine them all having hooves underneath, like something playful and devious out of a myth. They seemed anxious, too, like animals, shy as they approached him the way even the tamest animals can get sometimes when faced with the unfamiliar. There were three fans going, two small blue-bladed plastic jobs that swung side to side near the door, their slapping clatter echoing from the stone walls and the mirrors, and one big, tilting metal type that sat near the desk and blew straight at the guard's chest and head, so they had to come right up to the desk to talk to him without yelling. It struck him when they got there that they weren't really the yelling type. They addressed him politely, and never questioned that he couldn't let them into the building, even to look for someone. "If it's a real emergency," he offered, "you can call the cops. I can let them in." They didn't think that was necessary.

Instead he gave them the pen from the weekday visitors' log and tore a corner from one of the rearmost pages to write on. The smaller of the boys composed a note, folded it, put the name of the lady they were looking for on the outside, and then they left. The guard looked at the little folded note. In small writing, the sort he associated for some reason with men wearing bottle-bottom specs, it read *Inez Kunstler*. He set it under the corner of his lunch box so the fan wouldn't blow it away. They said good-bye as courteously as they had said hello, and left the guard to go back to his book.

The little man was anxious, too, when he came in, but aggressive about it, like a clockwork set so tight it just can't be still until the spring winds down. The door had swung open suddenly, in a rush, and planted him there, surrounded by a swirl of street noise, staring red-faced and heaving at the guard. His shirt was half untucked and covered in sweat and dirt and something that was probably blood. The guard let the little man stand there looking confused for a minute. Then, yelling to be heard over the noise, the guard said, "You just here for the fans, buddy? Or can I help you?"

"I need to get in," the little man yelled back in a high, rough voice. "I have to see someone."

The guard expected the little man to come closer, but he didn't, so he called back across the fan-rattled room, "There's a lot of different companies in this building, pal. You're going to have to be more specific." He waited while the little man searched his pockets and finally found a small piece of paper or something from which he hollered out a name. "You've got the right building," the guard answered, and the little man took a step forward, but he stopped short again when the guard continued, "but that office is closed."

The little man looked as if he didn't know the word. "Closed?" he yelled.

"Sure," the guard yelled. "Weekend. Everybody'll be back on Monday."

"I'm looking for someone working there now. Cleaning, I mean. She's there right now. She starts after people close. That's when she works."

"Listen. Why don't you come over here, so we can talk?" The little man approached, limping a bit as if he had hurt his ankle or his knee, although if he was in pain, his face didn't show it. His shirt was even dirtier when you saw it close up, and there was a rip down one side. "Shit, pal," the guard said. "You look like you've been through the wringer." The little guy didn't answer; he just looked past the guard to the two elevators at the back of the foyer. The guard said, "You call the cleaning company? They might know how to reach her."

The dirty little man was still looking towards the pair of elevators in the narrow hallway just behind. Then the little man said, "I guess I know how to find her."

"What was that?" the guard asked, even though he had heard clearly enough. It was just that he didn't like the way the guy had said it—and then there was something uneasy about the way the little man stood there, like he was anticipating something, and about the way the guy's eyes kept gliding past his own, that made the guard uncomfortable. Without thinking about it, the guard stood up, and finding himself standing he also found his hand gripped his belt in a way that let his thumb touch the wood butt of his pistol in its holster. "What time does your friend finish?" he said. "Maybe you can wait for her outside."

"I need to see her now. It can't wait." The little man started to walk towards the elevators. He didn't move fast, just the same limping pace at which he had crossed the room, but the guard knocked against the open drawer with his book in it, and all at once he was having to rush to get between the little man and the elevator doors. He banged against the little man as he moved past him and they both tensed up right away. The guard said, "Hey, I can't let you in there."

The little man looked up at him with this thin, blank stare. Then he made a sudden rush for the freight elevator. The guard had to grab and hold him back, press his whole body against the pushing. The man just kept pushing, moving to one side or the other as if the guard would somehow forget to follow him. Then the man was grabbing at him as if to yank him out of the way. The guard gave the little man a push that sent him falling backwards on his ass.

For a moment the guy just sat there on the granite floor, his face red but otherwise unchanged. The guard, enunciating carefully, said, "Mister, I haven't fired a gun at anything but a target since nineteen fifty-three, and I like it that way just fine, but you know they don't give me this thing for nothing." He had his whole hand on the gun butt now. The man started to get up, and the guard said to him, "Slowly," and he went slowly, standing finally with his back to the wall of the mirrored hallway. Over the man's shoulder the guard could see the two of them reflected again and again into the infinite distance.

The little man started tucking in his shirt, and the guard

took a breath. "It's an emergency," the little man said, finally, as if he were sharing a secret.

"Sure," the guard said. "Then it's easy. You call the cops. If they agree it's an emergency, it's open house. I let everybody in."

The little man simply said, "No."

They stood there for a while after that. His certainty about not calling the cops made the guard nervous, but he told himself that a man who doesn't like cops won't be quick to do anything that will get someone on the phone to them. He also noticed that the little man wasn't slipping his eyeballs around looking for the way past him any more, and he figured that was a good sign. He said, "Listen. First things first. Why don't you tell me her name?"

"Kunstler. Her name is Inez Kunstler."

"Her again?" The guard had spoken without thinking about it. He regretted it right away, too, because right away the little man became agitated.

"You know her?" the little man said.

"I'm starting to think she must be the most popular cleaning lady in New Jersey. I had a gang of hippies in here an hour ago asking for her."

"Did you let them in?" the little man asked anxiously. "Did he see her?"

"No," the guard said carefully. "Nobody saw her." The man nodded, and seemed maybe to relax a little. "And they were a lot more polite about it than you've been, I got to say. So I tell you what. I'll let you do what they did: you can write her a note. That's fair, right? But after that you have to leave or I'm getting the cops in here. This is trespassing, and if someone has to shoot you over it, I'd rather it be them."

He walked the little man back, a hand held up between

them, the two facing each other as if they were sharing a dance. The little man was still tense enough that his agitation was in the air. When they reached the desk the guard glanced quickly over at the weekday log and the open drawer. The only paper he could reach without having to stretch too far was the note the kids had left, held down by the lunch box. He pulled it free and held it out at arm's length. The little man put a hand out and for the first time the guard noticed the strange melted nubs of skin that were his two first fingers. "You can write it here on the back of the other one, okay?" he said.

The guy grabbed it, but instead of flipping it over, opened it while backing away. The guard had let himself get distracted thinking about where he had put his pen, and angry at himself as much as at the little guy, he barked, "Hey!" He rushed after the retreating little man, whose eyes were locked on what he was reading. The guard finally grabbed the paper away, but didn't get a good grip on it, so it fluttered to the floor. The little man looked at the guard briefly with his curious blank eyes, then down at the note. His lips were moving as if he were reciting something. The guard tried to think of what to say or do, but by then the little man was already heading for the door. The moment he reached the sidewalk, he began to run.

The guard waited for a minute, still on edge, in case he might come back. He walked to the front doors and looked through them at the street, then leaned down, took a ring of keys from his belt, and turned the lock that bolted to the floor. He wasn't supposed to lock up except for when he went to the dentist's office to use the toilet, but he needed it, at least for a while. He started back towards his chair. The note was still open on the floor. It was slightly twisted from being yanked around, shuddering sideways a little where it felt the underbelly of the fans' swinging wind. When the guard reached it he picked it up, smoothed it out, and read it. It said, "I'm sorry I wasn't home last night I have to talk to you Can you meet me when you're done?" There was an address. The guard folded it again and put it back in its place on the desk, under the same corner of the lunch box as before. He retrieved his book and sat down, but it was a while before he started reading.

From the moment he opened the scrap of paper and saw what was written there Kunstler repeated the address as once he had repeated to himself his own name, the drawn-out baptism of chanted repetition—*Abe Kunstler, Abe Kunstler, Abe Kunstler.* It carried with it the same edgeless hole of panic that had fallen through his rib cage when, a prelude to his life, he had answered the *help Wanted* sign and so was forced at last to become himself. Now it was the address that held both fear and the future, and he carved the same channel for it in his mind and body, made it the same function of his breathing. Asking a cabbie for directions had meant allowing the litany to rise up momentarily through his throat to his lips, and he worried briefly that by sharing it he might lose it, let it slip through his teeth into the world and escape. Kunstler listened and nodded as the cabbie waved his hands and chopped at the air: this many lefts and rights, that many blocks straight on— but he never let go of the words.

That was why after he had run with the sound coiled in his stitched and heaving chest through the streets from the office building, after he had rehearsed it across the cracked, sun-lashed sidewalk, driving one leg past the other in a torrent of ankle-twisting pain, he believed he could meet his body's command to stop at the bar. He could stand at the long wooden haven, he could fill himself with liquor, he could drink until his joints were loose; he would not forget. The lights flopping red and blue in the window were already like a promise of healing. Just to see them, just to step through the door and hear their neon buzz, was to feel the coming relief.

He knew then that there hadn't been any choice. He needed to retrieve his thinking, which was wrapped in a constricting dry gauze, unable to discern anything clearly. He almost counted on his fingers: the time minus the hours it would take Inez to get there. It didn't matter. He needed to take his drink and hope it unrolled in him a blueprint for deliverance.

The place was filling up, but Kunstler barely noticed anything, not the people or the space. In a kind of blindness he walked to a line of tall, fixed stools at the bar, climbed one, and asked the barman for whiskey. When the heavy little glass arrived he filled himself with the whole thing, a long thread of burning relief. As he waved for another his vision had already begun to clear, and he wondered if this was what it felt like the first time a man put on glasses, retooled to a crisper world.

The thoughts he needed didn't come, though. In the past somehow he had always known what to do: the name and the story that were the shape and image of the person he might become, the job giving that shape momentum and solidity, the girl Inez who was the light he shined blindingly in the eyes of anyone who might think to look at him twice. Hadn't he unerringly chosen the furnace and the knife, the short hair, the collared shirt? It was wanting the child that had been the problem. He had given in to the urge for something not needed. He had sold his safety to desire.

Now in his panic he would give it away again, this time to a swift parade of drinks, at the end of which he would lose control and the room spin around him as if he were a spindle, throw him roughly off his stool and against a wall of bare brick. Through the spinning he made out two men who held him by the arms as the bartender felt around for his pockets. Kunstler thought to himself, *I could have told them that the money's gone,* but then he realized that of course he already had. That was why they were checking: he had more liquor in him than he could pay for. He started to yell and then to struggle, but it was almost with a sense of obligation, because somehow his thoughts moved slowly, almost calmly, telling him, *Soon this will be over, since there's only so much pay they can get in blood and fighting.* It didn't surprise him that someone just as calmly said, "Heads up," when Kunstler's forearm came briefly loose and jerked like a piston in the emptiness. *If you can even call it a fight,* he corrected himself, kicking his legs and working his fist uselessly. He had to get the barman's hand out of his pockets, and even drunk he could calculate it was better they beat him than search him. At the instant in which his hand found a target, something soft and belly-like, Kunstler made out clearly his own reflection in the mirror behind the bar, a worn and dirty face nearly expressionless between two bottle necks. Someone hit the face and the reflection disappeared.

Then he was outside, where the sun was nearly gone but the heat still nestled in the pavement. He was facedown, and had to drag himself into some sort of consciousness through a head ringing and distant, a mind that floated softly within a far room of his own thinking. He tried to look around but his eyes crossed and swam. Over them was pressed a second image, shallow but indelible like a welder's spark, so that it was impossible to look away from it. It lingered even behind closed lids. Although he saw the buildings and the fading summer daylight and the cars, from deep inside the cage of his pain he found he was looking everywhere at a kitchen in a basement, at a light swinging violently, at a spreading lake of blood. The sharp knife from the kitchen was so near he could almost touch it, and the furnace door, and he had to fight to keep himself from reaching for what he knew he couldn't have. No amount of blinking would dissolve it.

It's him, Kunstler thought, meaning the man, a spirit come because after all this time his death was suddenly to have been for nothing, betrayed by the failure of the years between, by Kunstler's failure to make true the plan. He had promised and sworn to re-create the fallen husband, who had been lost already three times. He knew the man was lost every day again when not re-created in the boy, usurping and untrue. The boy: it was through his birth it had all been lost. All the nights and bars and drinks, all the men enticed, the hopes raised, the plans on which he had constructed his future, they had all disappeared like water gripped in a fist because of the boy. Now it seemed the man would be lost one final, irretrievable time when Kunstler, the vessel in which whatever remained of the man resided, was cracked open and emptied by the boy's disgusting words. *The sharp knife from the kitchen,* Kunstler kept thinking, his head oppressed by heat and fatigue and pain, spinning with the invitation of a blissful, thoughtless sleep—but in his far-off thoughts he still heard the sound of his own voice repeating silently the address, the words tattooed on his breath, and carried by the sound he made his way through the street towards the place, limping sightlessly, braced for the unknown task as he had braced himself long ago outside the door to the basement apartment, anticipating as then with a kind of relieved horror the dullness that he hoped would follow.

Then he was in front of the building on melting knees, making his way up the stoop even as he thought, *First in the war when his spirit was taken and his shell left empty but alive, then when the habit of living left across the slow dark kitchen floor, and last his body, part by part, the heat and blasting dust.* His right eye and cheekbone still shuddered from the punch he'd taken and now his eye was almost swollen shut. It stung with sweat but he didn't dare touch it. With a finger he tested the huge bump where the force of the blow had cracked his skull against the bar's brick wall. He thought of a head hitting a sink and of a head retreating from a thrown fist abruptly to a wall, and punching that head again now in his vision Kunstler was confused to see that the man he hit was himself. The sun was gone and in the dark the building seemed dead. The only lights he could see, faint, unfriendly, came from the top floor.

I'm too late, he thought. *She'll be there and I'm too goddamn late.* He could think of no other path, however, and now he was inside the building's narrow, unlit entryway, the smell of mold and summer garbage. Then he was on the stairs, and they creaked under him. He was suddenly so weak that he had to use his hands to pull himself up the steps. *Even my walk wants to give me away,* he told himself—although he could suddenly find no reason why he should sneak when they would see him soon enough. As he climbed he shook his throbbing head to clear from his eyes the kitchen and the furnace, the swinging bulb and the knife, but they wouldn't go. It was through them that he looked up towards the pale light at the top of the stairwell, and through them that he moved across the top-floor landing towards a door which nearly fell on him when he took the knob because it leaned loose against the wall. Beside it was an empty doorway.

Through that was a narrow hall. One end was brighter, and there was some kind of music. Kunstler passed more open doorways, but only one was lit, and he made his way there through the unmoving ghostly kitchen that rested behind his eye, the sharp knife always just beyond his hand. Then he could see a girl, a hippie girl. He could see her long and heavy hair, her thin shirt touched with sweat beneath the arms, her dirty bare feet, but he saw as well the spectral light that swung wildly over a half-remembered kitchen table after a final grab at life, and the pivoting shadows it threw across a lost room. Behind the girl a curly-haired boy looked out a dark window at the dark city, and over him spread the slow lake, fuel released from a uselessly spinning engine. The hippie girl was sitting at a table over which no bare light swung, and Kunstler knew this was wrong. Sitting with her were his wife and his child. Around them all the room rippled as if in water. One by one they all turned to look at him, the strangers first—her eyes calm, his dark and furtive—then the boy with his twisted face, and finally Inez.

"Has he told you?" Kunstler asked her. His voice was like a crushed tin can.

Inez stared at him, and began to rise from her chair. She said, "Abe, what are you . . ." The boy spoke, too, but Kunstler was already advancing on them, unlistening, in a body completely beyond his control, which moved and screamed demands, shook and clenched its fists and raised its arms in every gesture of violence, a body lashing out as it called again and again for an answer and then was pulled back and down by the others, the two strangers, their hands around him where for years no hands but only bandages had been, and he felt the ribbon of consciousness slipping from him, holding on to it just long enough to look up at the girl Inez a brief last time. He saw her as if from miles off.

——————————————— ○ ———————————————

She again now and no longer the he that once was, the he that had been presumed solid, had even at times seemed impenetrable, but was then torn open like a door to reveal beneath it the irrevocable, the treacherous and negating bones, the parts that were too deep for alteration to reach, that could never be exchanged. Hers was a body stripped bare even by the people who claimed they would save her, doctors and nurses who didn't understand that there were things to lose more important than the simple mechanics of life. She had been too weak to stop them from reducing her to a floating nameless thing, lost on an icy sea, and try as she might no haven would come to mind unless it was the dark and silent room where half a century before her father had called her "my girl" and finally breathed his life out.

How different it had been from the room where she was going to die, pastels and plastics and the endless vibrating half noise of the machines. And yet although here she would not find the dignity of silence, because there could be no dignity at all amid the chattering of the nurses and the doctors, the antiseptic they used to keep the stench away, this was where she would wait. She had awoken into an anticipation of the boy, a knowledge found in the air and nothing else: that wherever she was he would come. He couldn't fail her in that, at least. Where else was there to go, for any of them? They had no home any more, for by now they knew the secret that in fact was many secrets folded in upon themselves and fused, and their knowledge destroyed the unspoken thing that had been no less than her person, the one and indivisible fact of her, now dissolved like a snowflake caught and considered on the tip of a finger, so that she was destroyed, too, undone—and yet still the woman revealed was not the same she as had disappeared long ago, who now was and was not Kunstler, no longer and yet still the man who had never allowed himself the thought of comfort, who had put aside the hope of removing from his ear the years-long scream of fear that filled and isolated him.

She floated in an unmeasured waiting, knowing that time and the hospital sounds were nothing. The tubes and the bed and the machines, the metal trees that for fruit bore bags of blood: all these were nothing, as unimportant as the vanished name that once had been hers but was now forgotten, irretrievable. Their meeting would be as if they were in an empty room in an empty building, maybe on an empty earth, where this disappointment would peel everything else away and in the emptiness it left bring them together, and like the passage of the man her husband across the slow, dark lake, her own passage would have meaning because it, too, would somehow give life to a man, thinking, This is my body, but I will give it up for you.

How strange it was to learn only after all these years that it was at the moment of submission the man had been strongest, that he had been most what she admired when he appeared least like himself. Of course it was only in following the terrible road of his experience to its farthest post that she understood the distinguished, the majestic burden of transformation: a strength that abides in an acquiescence that is also a rebellion, a refusal to find value in the valued thing. That was true strength: to cast aside an average man's fortune of reduced potential in order to seize sovereignty over the future. She knew that she would give herself up to death and the boy not just so another could have what she had been gifted, but because in doing it she would demonstrate the immense power that came with her choice.

Suddenly the hospital was around her again. It was impossible to tell how long she had been there. She often went away from it into sleep, into the old wicked dream come again of the man her husband in his many parts waiting to be assembled but refusing assembly, and she unwilling to follow him, too afraid to sail after him across the lake of his death—until suddenly for once and for all time to come she wasn't, and at that moment she felt herself fly above his ruined body, rising finally into the moment of waking to the dark of the drawn curtain and the humming and buzzing of the hospital machines.

Someone was there. It had happened before, but this time she was sure: this time at last it would be the boy. It had to be, if only because she knew he would come, knew that he had to come before it was too late. She would rise when he came, closing her fists so he would have no choice but to fight when both would know that in her present weakness to fight would be her end, her release. So she started to raise her hand, because still she believed there was hope, and hoping she thought: if I am not a real man at least maybe in this last moment I will create one in the boy, offer him that strength of purpose that was not his other father's doing but mine, made by me and the tools of my hand, made as a machine is tooled. In that way maybe he will finally be my son, blood or no blood. I will raise my hand to deliver that weak blow that will bring about my own end, because underneath the long hair and flowered clothes, the stupid beads and feathers, maybe beneath that I have constructed a thing so solid that not even these distorted days of excess and confusion will take it from me.

He will not understand, not at first, what I am offering him, and yet because my treachery must appear all too deep and terrible, it will be unspeakable, and I know therefore he will not speak it, but only act, and in that we will at long last share a symptom, the results of a disappointment so great it cannot be ignored, and he will produce a swift retaliation, a gift delivered bare-handed and with the press of his flesh to mine, our final contact, the knock of bone on bone, the gesture by which power is transferred, the clenched fist that will call my thin, weak blood into compliant procession. In a way it will be our first and only true contact.

It would be the action of a man, she thought, one like the man her husband, the first man she had ever known to show true strength, and who had shown more of it when all else was stripped from him, when to pass his strength to another was all that remained. It was all that remained for her now, which is why when the figure came, perhaps the boy, silhouetted against the hospital's fluorescent light through the soft parting of the dark curtain, she began to raise her arm: not just to deliver the blow that she hoped would bring the fatal response, but because there was something she needed to show him. She needed to point him towards the future.

About the Author

Tadzio Koelb is a graduate of the prestigious writing program at the University of East Anglia. He has translated André Gide's work, and is an active reviewer and essayist for a variety of publications that include the *New York Times* and the *Times Literary Supplement*. He teaches writing at Rutgers University and lives in Brooklyn, New York.